FIREWALK

RACHEL HATCH BOOK FIVE

L.T. RYAN

with

BRIAN SHEA

LIQUID MIND MEDIA, LLC

Copyright © 2020 by L.T. Ryan, Liquid Mind Media, LLC, & Brian Christopher Shea. All rights reserved. No part of this publication may be copied, reproduced in any format, by any means, electronic or otherwise, without prior consent from the copyright owner and publisher of this book. This is a work of fiction. All characters, names, places and events are the product of the author's imagination or used fictitiously. For information contact:

contact@ltryan.com

http://LTRyan.com

https://www.facebook.com/JackNobleBooks

The authors wish to thank:
Amy, Barbara, Carol, Don, Gene, George, Karen, Kevin, Linea, Marty, Melissa, Rita, Stephanie, Steve, and William.

THE RACHEL HATCH SERIES

Drift

Downburst

Fever Burn

Smoke Signal

Firewalk

Whitewater (pre-order now)

RACHEL HATCH SHORT STORIES

Fractured

Proving Ground

The Gauntlet

ONE

HER RED HAIR was ablaze as the late afternoon sun filtered through the long, wavy curls. The bright tones of her hair complemented her pale skin exposed by a loose-fitting tank top. She looked like a porcelain doll on display. She downed the last bit of her drink and laughed at what the woman with her had said. Two men in a dark Toyota 4Runner watched her.

"It's a long drive. Might need to sample the goods before we get there. She's a fine piece of—" Trevor started, a thin smile etching across his face.

"Don't even think about it. You were lucky the last time. If they ever found out you touched the last girl, you and I wouldn't be sittin' here," Alejandro shifted in the driver's seat to face his cohort.

Trevor Fairmount, undaunted by the warning, stared out of the tinted windshield, licking his lips as though he had a T-bone steak in front of him and rubbing the bristles of his patchy beard.

Alejandro swatted the pony-tailed head of his partner, shocking him out of a daydream.

"What the hell was that for?"

"To snap you out of whatever stupid fantasy running through your sick mind." Alejandro's gaze hardened. "You touch this one and you won't have to worry about Mr. Carmen's muscle. I'll put a bullet through your thick skull myself."

"Don't act so high and mighty. What about that girl from Tulsa?" Trevor's face drew up into a sneer. "Because if I remember right, it was your idea to—"

"Shut up!" Alejandro turned away. The leather seat squeaked loudly in the silence that followed. "She was different. A throwaway."

Trevor shrugged, showing zero empathy. "They all seem the same to me."

"That's why you're still on the snatch-and-grab team."

"Uh, so are you."

Alejandro gripped the steering wheel with enough force that his knuckles whitened. He wanted to smack the back of his partner's head again. Or drive his fist into Trevor's bony face. The snide comment itself caused Alejandro's anger because of the truth behind it. He wanted this part of the job over with. Sure, his employer paid well, but he saw himself as more. He wanted to stop making these "runs."

For Alejandro Dominguez, this job was a chance for him to revamp his life. The two-time convicted felon had little chance of finding meaningful work. He'd tried, and he failed. But he had a particular skill that made him an asset to the organization. He was a good wheelman; that is why they recruited him.

He was bright, at least when he compared himself to his partner with whom they had paired him for the last year.

He despised Trevor, but there was little he could do about their partnership. It wasn't like he could go to HR and request a change. They were at the bottom tier of a much larger organization. But Alejandro aimed to prove himself worthy of a promotion. As long as he avoided messing with the merchandise and delivered consistently, he could move his way up to middle management and leave this despicable work to somebody else.

However, Alejandro was under no illusion that his partner would ever rise above his current status with the way he was ogling the redheaded teen at the bar. He was determined to make sure Trevor's hands remained to himself during their long ride to the border.

"What's with you lately, man? You're actin' like your shit don't stink. You know you're not better than me, you two-time loser."

I am better than you..., he thought. But he knew that was not the case. He had been justifying his mistake a thousand different ways.

He hated that Trevor had the nerve to bring up the castaway girl. It was a mistake. He'd been off his game that day. His girlfriend had just broken up with him and he took his frustration out on the inebriated girl they had been tasked with transporting.

Putting it out of his mind afterward, he attempted to bend the truth of its atrocity to make sense of what he'd done. He was angry at himself for showing weakness and giving in to his primal urges. Seeing the young, semi-conscious girl in the backseat compelled him to give in to Trevor's whim. Until now, they had never spoken of it. The fact Trevor felt the need to bring it up made him a liability. Something Alejandro needed to remedy.

When the cops caught him and threw him in Maricopa County's prison system for a botched bank robbery, his decision not to talk about his felony caught the eye of his current employer.

Mr. Carmen, who Alejandro had met once when he was first brought onboard, liked him for two important reasons. He could drive a car like no one else. And he could keep his mouth shut. In the underworld, those traits made him a rare commodity.

In the year he had provided his skills to the organization, he earned enough to upgrade his lifestyle. He moved out of the rundown efficiency apartment in the Maryvale subdivision of Phoenix. Prison did not leave him with much after his release, but he now owned a condo. He also bought himself a nice new ride. However, he never used his personal car for work purposes.

The organization rotated the vehicles for these types of transports. The license plates were legitimate, but no one could trace or verify the owners. The company took care of the logistics. All he had to do was drive. And keep Trevor's hands off the merchandise. The latter proved increasingly difficult.

His job was simple: Make the pickup, make the delivery, and don't get caught anywhere in between. These rules were harder than expected to follow. Since the team had added Alejandro, they never had to trade out drivers, and on this he prided himself.

He had come in as a driver one year ago, after they went through six drivers in less than three months. It was never openly talked about, but he assumed the drivers who had been "let go" did not go on to other careers. The rumors stated the other drivers were dead. In the criminal world, rumors usually carried as much weight as truth. Maybe more.

Alejandro Dominguez was not a killer. He had never fired a gun. In the underworld, not having pulled the trigger was a sign of weakness. So, whenever the topic came up in conversation, he never gave a direct answer. He quickly learned to be aloof enough to never confirm or deny. By leaving it open, the team concluded that part of Alejandro's criminal record involved murder. In a short period, Alejandro's imaginary body count grew with Trevor's imagination, and Trevor's big mouth spread the claims among the lower tier of the organization, giving Alejandro a certain status among them.

He never talked about his past, and he found it funny when his fictional backstory filled in. He corrected no one. As Trevor guessed about Alejandro's life prior to working for the organization, his fantasies of Alejandro as a cold-blooded killer became more vivid.

Alejandro secretly liked this power he had over his partner. While Trevor had openly admitted that he'd killed nobody, his resume was filled with "touching girls." Despite his onetime slip-up, Alejandro despised Trevor for his insatiable appetite for these young girls. Alejandro committed to stopping his partner from having a taste of the newest recruit. But he was not sure how to go about it.

Both men armed themselves per the protocol. But the way they had set up their snatch-and-grab system, they rarely used their guns as a method of intimidation. And they did not have to strong-arm these prized targets. They had other ways of enabling ease of transport when the time was right.

Alejandro watched as the dark-skinned brunette laughed and ordered another round of drinks. Alejandro knew her only as Cassandra. The organization had hired her multiple times in the past, at various locations. He enjoyed watching her work. She was by far the most attractive woman in the bar. He hoped to meet her outside of the parameters of work someday. He figured since the operation involved her, she would not judge him for his part in this criminal enterprise. He sipped his iced coffee and fantasized about a relationship with the full-lipped, dark-skinned Cassandra.

With her, it was always the third drink. Cassandra looked back from the bar to the patio table, where she and the redhead had spent the last hour. Alejandro knew one of the many ruses Cassandra would have used to get this girl to stay. Her favorite was playing the role of a star talent acquisitions agent. She once ran through her repertoire for Alejandro when he asked her how she did it. The ease with which she could coax these girls into submission amazed him.

She said it was simple. She understood the girls' needs and told them what they wanted to hear. Her star recruitment facade worked on many levels. What young teenage girl didn't want to see themselves in a TV commercial or movie? And she preyed on this desire.

She would approach her target, introduce herself, and provide a fake business card. She padded her resume by rattling off big-name directors and actors she had worked with in the past. She name-dropped casually to maximize authenticity. After gaining their trust, she would say something to the effect of, "But genuine talent... the real trick? Being yourself. The only way I'll know if you *really* have what it takes goes beyond beauty. I have to see the real you. Would you be willing to have a couple drinks and discuss opportunities?" This line or a variant thereof usually worked like a charm.

Once, about six months ago, Cassandra tried the line only to have it fail. This was a prime target. A client made a special request, offering a sizable down payment. Because Cassandra's charms were useless on this girl, Alejandro and Trevor had to come in as the muscle. It was the riskiest snatch-and-grab yet. It left Alejandro feeling exposed, and he never wanted to do that again.

It was easier when they were compliant, even if it was chemically induced, and that was what he was waiting for. He saw Cassandra make her move, only noticing because he knew what to watch for.

It was quick, a sleight of hand. As she leaned over to pay for the drinks, she dropped a crushed Rohypnol into one of them. The benzodiazepine dosage was high enough to incapacitate the girl within several minutes of ingestion. To onlookers, she would appear intoxicated. But it would limit her resistance and she would be more mentally malleable.

Cassandra walked back to the high-top table on the bar's patio where she had been talking with the young woman for the last hour. She handed the young redhead her third hard liquor drink, a Long Island Iced Tea. This drink was Cassandra's choice for the "young talent" she was "recruiting" because it masked the taste from the powder.

The drug also had an *anterograde* amnesia effect on its users. Once in the victim's system, it would render an inability to create fresh memories after amnesia set in. The drug created a chemically induced blackout. This was why it had become known as a "date rape" drug since it had the potential to erase any sexual trauma after ingestion. It would take longer for the Rohypnol to have its ultimate intended effect. There was also a dash of crushed Ambien to add an extra punch. By the time it kicked in, it would both wipe her memory and put her down for a long nap, which made for an easy commute.

Cassandra liked it because it would erase her face from their memory. Trevor liked it because it opened an opportunity for him to take advantage. Alejandro liked it because it made for a docile passenger for the long drive.

As intoxication took hold, Cassandra's charm really kicked in. She laid it on thick and told the redheaded girl about the money and the parties of all the famous people she'd helped. Then, as the young woman consumed her last drink of the early afternoon, Cassandra offered to take her to meet a big-time director. She would leave it on the table as a once-in-a-lifetime opportunity.

Cassandra set the tainted drink in front of the teen. She consumed it quicker than the first two. The buzz setting in. Her youthful body was not used to the high potency of the drink.

Alejandro watched the girl with the fire-red hair slide back in her chair ever so slightly. Her cheeks blushed and her eyes watered. She began fanning her face. The excitement at the prospect of meeting whatever director or producer seemed to delight her beyond words. She almost leapt from her seat with excitement.

Cassandra stood and ushered the girl towards the back of the patio area to the sidewalk. She hurried, but not so much so that the intoxicated teen couldn't keep up.

Alejandro noticed the teen starting to sway as the effects of the alcohol and drugs took effect.

The girl stopped for a moment and steadied herself, leaning against the wall. For a moment, she looked as though she was going to vomit. This would have been bad because if her body rejected the drug, she might have quickly come back to consciousness, complicating the plan. Alejandro did not like complications, especially when the unpredictable Trevor was sitting next to him.

Cassandra put a gentle hand on the teen's porcelain shoulder and asked her if she was okay. The girl nodded, and they proceeded around the corner and out of sight.

Alejandro started the ignition. The engine purred. He slipped the Toyota into drive and coasted around the corner.

Cassandra pulled out a cell phone and gave her last performance. She pretended to be on the phone with someone important. After hanging up, she told the almost incapacitated teen that her driver was on his way and would take them to a well-known director's house for a private meeting. Cassandra's talent for selling the false dream of this girl's first shot at being a star was nothing short of Oscar-worthy.

Alejandro pulled alongside the curb beyond where anybody from the bar could see. The teen leaned forward, teetering unsteadily, as she peered into the windows of the Toyota 4Runner's heavy tints.

Alejandro could hear Cassandra's voice as she said, "Hey, sweetie. Look, our ride's arrived." Her voice, smooth as velvet, rolled over her full lips. She opened the door to the backseat. The young girl looked at the two men inside. She froze and looked back at Cassandra, whose eyes were still warm and inviting. Even with the alcohol and drugs beginning to work their magic, fear spread over the girl's face.

"Don't worry, dear. They work for me, you'll see. They're true professionals. Now, slide on in."

The redhead hesitated a second longer before she did as she was told and slid across the rear black leather bench seat of the 4Runner. She positioned herself behind Trevor Fairmount. Her body slumped as she fought with her uncooperative mind to keep her head up.

Alejandro watched her in the rear-view mirror but did not turn to face her. He always found it better that these girls never looked directly into his eyes. It was unsettling, knowing what came next. Plus, the possibility of being identified later always kept him on edge. Through the mirror's reflection, he watched as the teen's head bobbed up and down loosely, like a bobblehead on the front dash of an 18-wheeler. The drugs and alcohol were fighting a winning battle moments before the girl would slip away into unconsciousness.

Cassandra looked at the girl one last time. "Oh, dang it. I forgot something back in the restaurant. Give me a quick second, hon. I'll be right back." She added, "Guys, keep the car running. I'll be right back." Alejandro felt Cassandra had overacted her part, but it didn't matter because of the girl's inebriated state. She nodded at Cassandra and tried to speak, but she slurred her words into an incomprehensible series of sounds. The one discernable word in her sentence was "wait."

Cassandra closed the door and walked away.

Alejandro pressed the automatic lock on the driver's side armrest and activated the child locks and windows.

The girl's eyes widened, offering the last bit of resistance as Trevor turned in his seat to face her. In less than twenty seconds, he handcuffed and gagged her. She slumped to the side. Her head came to rest against the rear passenger door.

As her eyes rolled into the back of her head, Alejandro drove toward the next waypoint in the girl's journey.

TWO

HATCH LOOKED at the gas gauge of her rental, a gray Ford Focus hatchback. The gas level indicator had just crossed the boundary of the quarter-tank range. She let no vehicle get below that. Old habits die hard. She never let herself be in the position of running out of fuel. It happened to her once overseas. The experience left her cautious. A ten-mile trek with a full combat load out in a combat environment would ingrain that habit in anyone. In that case, the gas gauge had been damaged.

She had been in Arizona for the past several hours of her drive, having just merged from the 303 with I-10 for a quick dogleg around the western outermost edge of Phoenix. She took exit 114 and followed the signs directing her to a Gas-N-Sip station at the corner of Miller Street, across from a Charlie's Chicken restaurant. The billboard in the lot advertised fresh, hot chicken available twenty-four-seven. Hatch thought it funny that somebody at 3 or 4 a.m. would need chicken, but it made sense. This area was a major route for truckers, their circadian rhythm off by the all-night driving. A three in the morning chicken snack would be lunchtime for them.

Hatch, when working patrol in her early years as a military police officer, had worked the midnight shift. For the first two years as a new enlistee, they had assigned her to nights. Early on, she found the change tough, but once she had grown accustomed, she found it equally tough to shift back to the more normalized hours of the day shift.

She pulled to a stop at pump number four. There was one other pump in use by a large, dark-colored SUV parked on the other side at pump three. She noticed the driver stayed inside with the engine running. She could barely discern any facial features through the heavy tint of the glass. The driver did not seem to notice or care about Hatch's arrival at the Gas-N-Sip.

She headed toward the gas station's mart as she preferred to prepay for her gas in cash. Less chance of a trail.

Ever since leaving Hawk's Landing for the last time, she was extra cautious about her movements. Before departing, she structured her bank account to filter her money through her mother's checking account. She listed her mother as the beneficiary so she would receive fifty-five percent of Hatch's military retirement for the rest of her life. Although it was a dip in income from what Hatch received when she was "alive," it was more than enough when coupled with the payout of her two-hundred fifty grand life insurance policy. Having the money in her mother's account provided Hatch with a steady flow of income until she could find her way in the unknown world. Her unknown world.

She figured based on the size of the car's tank that twenty-five dollars would be enough to fill up for the next couple hundred miles until she got closer to her destination, Coronado, California. The Gas-N-Sip was almost halfway between Hawk's Landing and Coronado.

That she was hovering between a past life—now dead and buried—and an uncertain future was not lost on her. She had a long list of questions for her former boyfriend, Alden Cruise. Her first question, how was he able to give her advance warning before the hunter-killer team from Talent Executive Services had made her a target?

He'd sent her the message: *Come to where the moon kisses the sea.*

It was a reference to their first date. He'd taken her to Naval Amphibious Base, across the way from where BUD/s, Basic Underwater

Demolition/SEAL training, took place. They sat out by the bay and talked for hours. The moon was cartoonishly big as it hovered above the bay's calm, dark water. She verbalized the scene with, "It's as if the moon is kissing the sea." A nice memory, untainted by time.

To the hired guns at Talon Executive Services, she was dead. Hopefully, the story and evidence trail created by Savage would keep them believing she was dead. Hatch had taken several precautions since leaving Hawk's Landing to make sure that if they conducted any residual follow-up, all roads would lead to nowhere. She took drastic measures to fake her own death and further protect her mother, niece and nephew, and Dalton Savage from any fallout. She would look over her shoulder for the rest of her life, but she gave her family the chance of not having to do the same.

As she crossed the sunbaked asphalt toward the store, the entrance door opened. She was close enough to feel a shift in the oppressive hot air as the overworked air conditioner inside labored.

A man and teenage girl exited. The duo didn't match. The man was scraggly. He was thin with a thick goatee. His gaunt face was punctuated with two beady eyes which held a wildness like that of a feral cat. The girl could have been seventeen, no more than eighteen. Her bleached blonde hair and sun-kissed skin contrasted with her white collared shirt and short plaid school dress. There was a maroon and gold emblem embroidered above her left breast, and a gold pin on her collar caught the sun's light.

The girl made eye contact with Hatch for a brief second. Hatch caught something, but she wasn't sure what it was. She noticed the man tighten his grip around the teen's elbow as Hatch approached. It was a barely perceptible tension in the goateed man's hand. But Hatch noticed.

As they passed, the girl's eyes cast downward.

Hatch caught herself wondering about the girl, looking for deeper meaning in the eye contact that they had made. Hatch was in a mental battle with herself as she tried to make sense of what she had seen in the girl's eyes. The man with her, his tight grip, the driver waiting in the idling SUV. Everything was off. But Hatch stopped herself cold.

She told herself to stop looking at everything as a giant threat. It was so hard to dismiss her perceptions after fifteen years of military service. Maybe the world wasn't a big, scary place. Maybe not everybody was a threat. Maybe not everybody was a victim. Was everything she looked at now going to be tainted by years of heartache and tragedy?

She gave a lot of thought to her understanding of the world away from the battlefield. She never took the time to see the normalcy of life, or at least a normal that others could understand. Circumstances had dictated a different course, and she realized it, and anyone who knew her understood her jaded perception.

Still, seeing the girl raised the question, was she in trouble? Hatch struggled for the answer. As a person who took pride in making split-second life-and-death decisions, she was now at odds.

She looked for a plausible excuse why the girl may have looked scared or downtrodden. Why did the man escorting her shuffle her along more quickly when he saw Hatch? Maybe it was his niece? Maybe he was overprotective? The girl looked woozy and off-center. She might've gotten car sick and they had pulled off at this station to allow the girl an opportunity to use the bathroom. Her interpretation of the goateed man's grip on her elbow might have been his effort to support her unsteady gait. She looked peaked.

The goateed man did not hold the door for Hatch as she approached. He moved swiftly across the parking lot toward the idling SUV. Hatch caught the door right before it closed and pulled it wide again. As she entered the air-conditioned interior of the gas station, she looked back at the girl one more time.

The girl looked at Hatch. Her eyes flashed. Hatch recognized it. This time there was no doubt in her mind. The fog of her momentary internal debate lifted. It was fear. Even in the clouded malaise the girl was under, her eyes remained defiant.

As the door closed, Hatch saw the girl's hand flick something out onto the ground. The goateed man didn't notice as he slipped into the passenger seat and the vehicle pulled away.

THREE

HATCH STOOD for a moment and watched the vehicle exit the parking lot. She held the door ajar and feeling the air conditioning cool her warm skin. The SUV did not speed away in any attention-drawing fashion, but there was an urgency to the departure.

Before letting the door shut on her, she turned and walked to where the girl had been moments before. The SUV was now out of sight. It slipped into traffic and disappeared down the road towards the interstate.

She scanned the ground where the girl had dropped the small item at the last moment. With the sun overhead in the cloudless sky, she saw a golden glimmer alongside the cracked curbing of the raised concrete island of the pump. There beside a crushed cigarette butt laid a shiny gold pin. The one she'd seen on the girl's collar. She picked it up and examined it. The sun had already warmed the metal. It was about the size of her thumbnail and was shaped like a shield. The words Academic Achievement were scrolled across the top and in its center a golden genie's lamp. She turned the pin over. On the back was an H and A. Hatch wasn't sure the meaning. Maybe H A was a monogram? The girl's initials?

15

The girl had put in the effort to remove the pin from her collar and drop it after she made eye contact with Hatch. She left Hatch a message.

Hatch ran back to the convenience store. She moved through the threshold of the air-conditioned space and a chime rang when her legs crossed the infrared door sensor at the entrance.

A floppy-haired kid, no older than twenty-one, looked at Hatch with worry as he came in from the back door of the store. Before the employee exit closed, Hatch caught a glimpse of a car pulling away. The attendant had a wad of cash bunched up in his front pocket.

He eyed Hatch and she him. She knew what she had just witnessed. The clerk had sold drugs out of the back of the store. A pretty good front for a dealer, using the back entrance of a highway gas station to sell. Cops would not notice a car pulling up at a gas station and leaving.

But Hatch noticed. It was the $20 bill sticking out of the corner of his pocket that confirmed the exchange had been made and that he was the seller. Maybe weed, but she didn't smell the distinct scent of cannabis. It was likely harder, meth, or maybe cocaine. From the look of the attendant, she guessed meth.

She asked him with urgency, "I need to see a recording from your surveillance cameras. You have a system above the pumps, yes?"

"What's it to you? What are you, a cop or somethin'?" The attitude stretched across his face, his oily skin in that phase of pubescent growth prior to manhood. Probably contributed to by a poor diet. Whatever drugs he was selling, and most likely using also, contributed to his ruddiness.

"It doesn't matter who I am. I need to see that videotape now."

"Lady, if you're not the cops then you got no business tellin' me what to do, 'cause I ain't gonna do it."

Hatch stopped for a second. He had a point. She wasn't law enforcement, but she used to be. She knew the lingo. Maybe that's what he picked up from her when she'd first walked in. It wasn't long before the clerk, wearing the nametag labeled Jimmy S., discerned that she was not actively employed with any law enforcement agency. Her last opportunity for that disappeared in Hawk's Landing.

Had she been a cop, the badge would have already been on display and would have mitigated any further resistance from the creep. He must have assumed this as well and was now firming his resistance.

"Let's go over this again. I need to see the videotapes of that pump. The one where the SUV just took off from."

"Pump three?"

"Yes. Pump number three."

"I'm going to need to see your badge or something, if you--"

"I didn't say I was law enforcement, but I will tell you this: if I don't see that footage in the next thirty seconds, I will call the police. And trust me. They're also going to want to see that recording. And they will want a full statement from both of us. And I may be inclined to mention that I watched you come in from the back of your store with a wad of cash, having completed a drug transaction."

"Hey lady, I didn't--" he tried to interrupt.

Hatch dismissed this feeble attempt. "I guarantee you if they bring a canine here..." She let the threat hang in the air. Jimmy made a subconscious glance to a lockbox behind the counter, giving away the location of his stash. "They're going to find your stash and take your money. You'll lose your job and they'll arrest you. Or you can turn around, take me to the office or wherever you keep your video surveillance, and pull up the footage of the SUV. It's your choice."

"I don't have to do anything you tell me." He tucked the exposed cash deeper into his pocket and stared at Hatch with attempted intimidation. It didn't work. Hatch smiled back, unnerving the boy further.

"Listen, there's another way this can go down without phone calls. I could walk back there and pull the tape myself, but I prefer your cooperation."

Jimmy looked towards a closed door near the rear of the store, then back at Hatch as if he could stop her from going in.

"You can't do that, lady."

"Or what? You'll call the police? I already told you that was option one. And if you try to stop me, well then, I'm sure I could find another option. But that one is going to leave you hurt. Look, life is full of choices and I'd say this one matters. So, choose wisely."

She was wearing a short-sleeve shirt. Her time in Africa had taught her not to feel the shame of her scars, but she was still learning to be comfortable in her own skin. Jimmy now noticed the scar tissue trailing down her arm and intertwining with the tattoo. He was processing Hatch. And if her perception was correct, she saw him quiver. The rough exterior of the boy who was attempting to intimidate fell away.

"I don't want any trouble, lady."

"Neither do I. All I want is to see the video."

He was quiet. She could tell he was worn down by the exchange. He must have run through the options she provided. None of them registered as ideal, but he would seek to find the path of least resistance. Getting beat up by a female or turned over to the cops was not high on his priority list.

"Fine. I'll show you the damn tape. But then you get out of my store. Got it?"

"Absolutely. After you put twenty-five dollars in pump number four for me."

He looked flustered and angry, but then resigned himself. She laid the cash on the counter. Jimmy moved behind the register and pushed a button, activating the pump.

"Okay. Now the video," she said.

He walked back out from behind the counter and led Hatch toward the closed door with the sign "Manager," affixed to it.

"You know, I could get fired for this." He opened the door.

"I'm pretty sure they should fire you."

He entered without further resistance and plopped himself into the office chair. The curved backing of the black chair was held together by silver duct tape. Three of the four rollers worked as he scooted forward with a loud squeak of the fourth. After a few strokes on the keyboard, he activated the camera system over pump number four. Using a dial knob, he rewound the taped surveillance to where the SUV pulled up to a stop.

"Stop there," Hatch said. She watched for a moment. "I need a pen and a piece of paper."

He rummaged through the desk's disorganized top and found both. She jotted down the license plate, and the vehicle's make and model. "All right, run it."

He ran the tape as Hatch watched carefully. The driver got out and worked the pump. The passenger remained in the seat for a moment, then exited. He unlatched the girl from the back. *She couldn't even undo her seatbelt*, Hatch thought. *What the hell did they give her?* Whatever was wrong with the girl, she was clearly incapacitated.

Hatch watched her as the goateed man guided her into the store. Right before the door opened, he whispered in her ear. A threat Hatch presumed.

"Did they buy anything?"

The kid shook his head. "Just the gas. Those two went into the back. She had to use the bathroom."

"He went with her into the bathroom?" Hatch interrupted.

"No. He stood outside though like he was guarding her. Pretty girl like that, I guess you got to protect 'em."

Hatch ignored Jimmy's musings. "Did they say anything? Did you hear her talk? Did she try to communicate with you?"

"Not that I noticed."

"And then what?"

"They left. You came in. That's about it."

"Have you seen them in here before? Have you ever seen her? The goateed man? The man at the pump?"

He shook his head. "Never seen them before in my life."

She looked at him before taking one last look at the occupants of the SUV. She took out her flip phone and snapped a photograph of both men and the girl.

"I hope for your sake you never see *me* again," Hatch mumbled to herself, but realized Jimmy must have thought the comment was meant for him. She offered no explanation to the contrary.

She walked out into the sun, filled her tank, and drove off in the same direction as the SUV.

FOUR

HATCH HELD the smartphone in her hand. She thought of her nephew Jake and his love of technology. She wished he was there to see she'd upgraded beyond the flip phone to the modern era. The phone had a prepaid data plan, paid for in cash and registered to a name that was not hers. For all intents and purposes, it was a burner phone. The usage of which would be untraceable to Hatch in her new life.

She punched in the information using the one-finger hunt and peck method of entering the query into the search bar. Hatch hadn't figured out how to use the rapid fire two-thumb method of typing. She doubted she ever would.

It didn't take her more than a couple minutes before she found what she was looking for. She searched for schools beginning with H and narrowed the results by limiting the scope to the area around Phoenix. Harrison Alton Preparatory was at the top of the list. Hatch accessed the website. She scrolled through and found several pictures of students advertising the variety of extracurricular activities offered. The colors of the uniforms were purple and lime and black, not the same outfit the girl at the gas station had been in.

Hatch continued her search. Third from the top was Horton Academy. She clicked on the link. The maroon and gold banner scrolled across the top of the webpage. "Horton Academy: Where Excellence Exceeds Expectations." The colors were identical to that of the pin the girl had dropped. There were pictures of students milling about common areas of campus and they were wearing the same uniform as the girl. She scrolled down the page until she found the address and phone number, but not before eyeing the price of tuition. It cost over twenty thousand dollars a year to attend the preparatory high school. That was more than Hatch made during her first year in the Army.

Hatch considered calling, but she decided she'd be able to get a better read on the situation if she were to visit in person. Another few taps on the screen and Hatch mapped her drive. While there was a convenience to smartphones, she still preferred taking out a Rand McNally Road Atlas and plotting her course. But the technology in her hand did in seconds what would take her several minutes. And if Hatch's gut instinct was right, every second counted.

It wasn't that Hatch was against technology. Up until this point in her life, she hadn't seen the need for it. She kept her life simple, but after leaving Hawk's Landing for the last time, she decided having access to a wider breadth of information made her feel closer to the home to which she could never return. Jake would have been proud of her for navigating the web with ease and not needing his help.

Hatch recalled the family she'd left behind and wished things could be different. She wished she were looking over Jake's shoulder while he trained. Hatch longed to hear Daphne's silly ramblings as she narrated her next crayon masterpiece. Their voices echoed in her mind. She feared that over time the sound would fade altogether. The short period in which she'd been away felt like a lifetime. As if waking from a lucid dream into a new life, a life she didn't want—a life without a sense of self, devoid of purpose. To the world, Hatch was dead. To her family, she was a ghost. A sacrifice made with the sole intent of keeping them safe and out of harm's way.

She pushed her family back into the recesses of her mind and set out for the address on her phone.

THE DRIVE WASN'T TOO long distance-wise. Phoenix traffic turned a twenty-minute drive into shy of an hour to get to the campus. The visitor parking lot was adjacent to a high wall with gated access. Hatch parked, exited, and approached the school's visitor entrance. Spotting an external call box with an attached phone marked with a sign: Visitors Must Call Main Desk.

Hatch picked up the receiver and listened as the phone system auto-dialed the main desk. It rang once before being picked up.

"Horton Academy. How may I help you?" a woman's voice asked from the other end.

"I'd like to speak with someone regarding a student's attendance," Hatch said.

"Are you a parent or guardian?"

"No." Hatch assumed there were protocols in place to vet visitors and ensure they had a reason to be on campus. She added to her answer, realizing the need to better explain herself. "I have concerns about the safety of a student from your school."

There was silence from the other end. Then came a loud buzzing sound from the locked pedestrian gate nearby. "Follow the signs through the courtyard. The main office will be on the right."

Hatch pressed the gate's handle and the door opened. She stepped inside the walled expanse of the academy. If Hatch didn't know better, she would've assumed she was on a college campus. Several students moved about the main space. She must have entered during a class exchange. Hatch noted that all students were wearing the maroon skirt and gold-collared shirts of the academy's dress code.

There was a meticulously landscaped common space acting as a center point with stone paths leading off in seven different directions. They designed the surrounding buildings in Mediterranean revival with a heavy Spanish influence. The white of the thick stucco clad walls bounced the mid-morning sun's light off in a blinding fashion, causing Hatch to squint. The one-story buildings lined the surrounding area of the courtyard, allowing the hilly backdrop to remain visible in the distance.

She followed the dark stained hand-carved wooden sign's directions to the main office. As she entered, a woman seated at the front desk with short black hair and a nose that curled up like a ski jump looked up. The plaque centered on the desk read: Ms. Watkins, Executive Administrative Assistant.

Fancy title for a fancy place.

Watkins cradled the lime-green phone receiver, her chin holding it against her shoulder like a vice grip. "You wanted to talk about a student?"

"Yes. I'd like to speak to whoever oversees attendance."

"May I ask who you are?"

Hatch heard the underlying tone. This gatekeeper to the school wasn't asking Hatch for her name—she was demanding it. Hatch realized she didn't have one to give. Rachel Hatch was dead. She couldn't be poking her nose into things and using her own name, so she formed a new one on the spot, combining a little girl she loved more than anything and a man who'd saved her life. "I'm Daphne Nighthawk."

The secretary picked up a clipboard with a pen tied to the top and slide it across the countertop to Hatch. "I'm going to need you to sign in."

Hatch did a sloppy rendering of her new pseudonym and handed it back.

Watkins was on hold, annoyed at whoever was on the other end of the phone and at Hatch's interruption. Hatch guessed, after hearing the direct nature of the woman on the intercom and then seeing her in person, that the annoyance was nothing personal. It appeared to be Watkins' natural demeanor, which lacked any bedside manner. But efficient people were sometimes void of such. Hatch hoped she could answer the question she had.

After several seconds, Watkins finished the phone call and hung up. She looked up at Hatch and eyed her damaged right arm. Hatch had become accustomed to people's shock at her height and athletic build. And the scars. But this woman said nothing. She eyed her, unimpressed.

"I'm interested if you could tell me if there's any student missing or absent that has not been excused?"

"What's your relation to the student?"

"I have none. I'm a concerned citizen trying to check on the wellbeing of a student."

Watkins seemed put off by this and tapped the eraser end of a pencil against her chin. "Well, why don't you start by telling me the student's name?"

"I can't do that."

Watkins let out an exasperated sigh. She leaned forward and raised an eyebrow. "Then I probably can't help you."

Hatch now understood the real value of Ms. Watkins, Executive Administrative Assistant. She was a guard dog for the school and probably did a good job keeping parents, faculty, and students in line. But her bulldoggish manner had zero effect on Hatch.

"It's not that I don't want to tell you." She released her own exasperated sigh. "I don't know her name."

"I assumed that you were a relative or family friend, but now I do not understand why you are here."

"Listen, I'm concerned about the safety of one of your students. I found this." Hatch held out her hand, exposing the Academic Excellence lapel pin. "Does this belong to your school? It had the H.A. embossed on the back and I assumed that this is where it came from."

Watkins eyed it and then look back at Hatch, giving a slight nod of her head. "It is."

"A girl dropped it and I wanted to return it."

"But that's not what you asked," Watkins' voice carried with it an air of suspicion. "You found a lapel pin and came here to return it?"

"I saw a girl wearing this. She looked distressed and dropped it. I don't know if she was trying to signal me. But something was off. I wanted to see if there are any unexcused absences. I want to make sense out of what I saw."

"Well, what did you see?"

"I told you—" Hatch took a moment to lower her voice—"a girl in distress who looked at me and dropped this. She left it behind for me to find. I figured if I could come here and figure out who she was then—"

Watkins interrupted, "Are you working with law enforcement? Are you a private investigator?"

"I'm neither. I'm a concerned citizen." Hatch stuffed the lapel pin back into her pocket. "That's got to account for something."

"I can't divulge any of our students' information to somebody walking in off the street. You understand this, I hope?"

Hatch understood but still hoped she could get somewhere with this woman. "I'm asking if you know of anyone that is missing."

"Why don't you describe her to me?" Watkins asked.

"I guessed the girl to be seventeen, maybe eighteen. She had blonde hair, tan skin, athletic build, short—shorter than me."

Watkins diverted her attention from Hatch to her computer screen. Her fingers flew across the keyboard with lightning speed. Hatch couldn't see the monitor so she tried to adjust herself in hopes that she could catch a glimpse, but Watkins turned the screen out of eyesight.

"I'm sorry, Miss Nighthawk, but there's nothing I can do for you."

"You're not the least bit concerned? I'm telling you that one of your students was at a gas station over an hour away from here and she looked like she was in trouble. How are you not helping me—helping her?"

"By policy, I cannot release any of this information to you directly, no matter how good your intentions. You're more than capable of calling the police if you'd like, and maybe they can help."

"Right now, all I need to know," Hatch steadied herself, "is whether this girl is in trouble. I need to know if she is absent, excused, or missing."

Hatch realized she had uncharacteristically raised her tone. Both had an equally important stance to hold the line. Watkins was concerned about divulging information to a woman who had no business asking. And Hatch was determined to find out if this girl was in trouble.

Off to the right, rifling through mailboxes, was a short mouse-like teacher. She was reading through pamphlets left in her mailbox and looked over at the exchange. Hatch could feel her gaze and turned to face her. The schoolteacher was nearly a foot shorter than Hatch and squat, like a tomato. Whatever Hatch had in height; the teacher matched in width. She had blotchy cheeks and wild curly hair that shrouded her face. Through the curls she made eye contact with Hatch. This woman knew something. But with Watkins being the lineman, protecting all information regarding the school like a star quarterback, it wasn't the best place and time to ask her.

"All I need is a name," Hatch said. "Give me the girl's name and I can take it from there."

"I'm sorry. School policy does not allow me to release any information about our students to anybody but the parents, legal guardians, or somebody appointed by the parents or legal guardians. To do anything else would cost me my job. And I'm sorry Miss Nighthawk, but I've known you for all of two minutes and for me, it's been two minutes too long. So, I'm going to ask you kindly to leave, and if you have any further concerns, you can bring them up with the Hermosa Valley Police Department. And I'm sure they'll be in contact with me." She squinted her eyes in a taunting manner, almost challenging Hatch.

Hatch bit the inside of her lip, knowing she'd reached an impasse with Ms. Watkins. Hatch cast a last look back at the squat teacher, who was still eavesdropping, before turning and walking out the door.

As the door was shutting, Hatch heard it swing open again before coming to a complete close. Hatch continued walking without looking back, ensuring she was out of sight of the main office's window before turning to face the squat teacher approaching.

"Excuse me," the teacher said. Her voice squeaked like a mouse. "I don't mean to pry, but I couldn't help overhearing."

"Do you know who I'm asking about?" Hatch asked.

The teacher bobbed her head. "Her name is Kaitlin Moss."

Hatch stopped. "How long has she been absent from school?"

"Two days."

"If there's a concern, why wouldn't Watkins offer any help?"

The small teacher fanned her arm out at the impressive exterior of the Horton Academy School. "This is an extremely affluent community, and this school holds some of the Phoenix area's richest children. When

Kaitlin went missing, the family hired a private investigator to assist, not satisfied that law enforcement was adequately handling the job. The initial media coverage brought out a bunch of crazies looking to offer their assistance in the hopes of recouping a monetary reward for locating her."

"I didn't realize," Hatch muttered.

"You've never heard of Kyle Moss?"

Hatch shrugged. "Not really up on the rich and famous."

The teacher seemed taken aback. "You've heard of Sentinel Security, right?"

Hatch shrugged again. "I'm not from around here. But I get it, the Moss family's got money."

"That's an understatement. Kyle Moss is one of the school's biggest benefactors." The curly haired teacher jutted her chin toward a domed building across the courtyard. The Kyle Moss Observatory. "Beyond that, the Academy is extremely protective. And Mr. Moss made a point with the headmaster about minimizing any exposure to only the family. Ms. Watkins feared you were prying. She's under a strict policy not to release information. She would lose her job. That wasn't a lie." The teacher leaned in closer to Hatch and lowered her voice. "And she was rude as she can be trying to do what she believed was in the best interest of the child."

"Well, at least the police are already involved. It'll make it easier when I speak with them."

"They are, but in Hermosa Valley the police aren't really known for handling major crimes. There isn't a huge crime rate in this area. And for what crimes happen, they work hard to make them disappear. It's more about protecting the image of the town. That's why the family hired a private detective."

"How do I go about getting ahold of him?" Hatch asked.

"I'm not sure. I guess you'd have to contact the family."

"I have to ask, why are you telling me all of this?"

"The cops came through here yesterday and spoke to teachers and students who had any contact with Kaitlin. I'm her English and first period homeroom teacher. I told the cops everything I knew about her routine and the friend she hangs out with. I know they questioned a lot of people, but nobody knows anything. You're the first person I've seen who has any information regarding her whereabouts since she disappeared and from what I overheard you saying, she may be in danger."

"That's what I'm trying to figure out," Hatch said. "Thank you."

The clock inside Hatch's head began to tick. Real or imagined, the timeline for finding Kaitlin Moss was already in motion. Having learned that Kaitlin had been missing for two days, Hatch realized she was way behind the power curve. She set out toward the exit.

"I hope you can help her," the squat teacher called out.

Hatch slowed but didn't stop, turning slightly and speaking over her shoulder. "I'll do my best."

"She's a good kid. One of the smartest girls I've taught. I have high hopes for her. She had plans of Harvard in the fall. She's kindhearted to a fault. Maybe that's how she got into this trouble. She would do anything to help somebody in need. Maybe she got mixed up with the wrong people."

Hatch thought about her own code, about how she believed in putting the benefit of others ahead of herself. "Good people deserve protecting," Hatch said softly, but loud enough for the short teacher to hear. "And I'll promise you one thing, I'll do my very best to bring her home."

Hatch continued to her car. She sat for a second, allowing the Ford's air conditioning to battle back against the rapidly increasing heat before pulling out her phone and punching in the address to the Hermosa Valley Police Department.

As she pulled out of the Horton Academy visitor lot, she decided her trip to Coronado was going to have to wait.

FIVE

THE SLAM of a car door woke her up. Her nostrils were assaulted by a pungent odor, the air surrounding her smelled of urine. She tried to reach out in the darkness, but her arms didn't cooperate. They were tied behind her back. She made a more concerted effort to move, again met by resistance. This time, a pinching pain at her wrists accompanied the movement. As the world around her came into view, she realized she was lying on her side in the backseat of a vehicle. As she worked herself into a seated position, she noticed the dampness of her jeans and shamefully realized the source of the urine smell came from her. She didn't know whether to be embarrassed or terrified. She was leaning hard toward terrified.

"What the hell?" The slur of her words surprised her. The effort it took to sit left her feeling dizzy. She fought against the urge to vomit.

There was one point of reference she had in her seventeen years of life where she'd felt like this before. When she was fourteen, she snuck into her parents' liquor cabinet. She didn't remember much after the fourth rum and coke she'd made. And the hours after were permanently erased from her memory. What she did remember was the following morning being woken up by the screams of her mother after seeing her passed out on the kitchen floor in a pool of her own vomit. Her father told her later that she was lucky she didn't die. The following twenty-four hours of recovery made her wish for death. Her current physical and mental status rivaled that memory. The handcuffs on her wrist were an unwanted x-factor.

The world around her spun. She half wondered if it was all a bad dream. Her mind was feverish, half conscious with the understanding of her current reality coupled with a distortion of memory as to how she got here. Wherever here was.

She searched her mind for any trace of memory to make sense of her circumstances. The confusion of putting reason into the gap of time overwhelmed her. She shook her head, hoping it would lift the fog, but the only thing it did was worsen the spins. As her stomach wretched, she remembered the bar.

Dammit! She gritted her teeth, angry at herself. She worked her hands around to her back-left pocket, where she always kept her iPhone. Gone. So was her ID, cash, and keys. She was most angry about the cash. She had worked extra hours at the consignment shop to earn that money, and now it was gone. There was no way she spent the hundred dollars she took with her to the bar. But it wasn't in her pocket. *I've been robbed. Where's my phone?* Her shackled hands ran along the cushion, but the blind search yielded nothing.

She had nothing except her urine-soaked clothes. The dampness of which sent a chill across her body. With each passing second, the wooziness in her head ebbed ever so slightly. No amount of mental effort answered the question of how she had gotten here. The last thing she remembered was the bar, and the handsome guy who had been talking to her. She hadn't had a guy show her that kind of interest in a while, and she remembered liking the attention. All courtesy of her older sister's ID. She'd passed the bouncer's perusal of her credentials and had gotten into the bar, the first time she'd ever done it. Thanks to her friend Julie's endless persistence. Her sister was going to kill her when she found out she lost the ID.

She needed her phone like a junkie needed a fix. That phone was her connection to everything. It was a hand-me-down from her sister. Everything in Angela's life was. She was desperate to call Julie to find out what happened and to see if she had gotten home safe. Angela kicked herself for letting her friend leave without her.

Julie had pleaded, trying to convince her to leave. But the woman she'd been talking to had been so captivating. Her name fluttered across her mind. Cassandra. She spoke with an accent. Other than that, she couldn't remember much else about the conversation or what led her to the here and now. Angela remembered following her to a car. She remembered the driver's eyes being the deep brown of finished mahogany. His perfectly sculpted jawline seemed to soften when he smiled. His movie star good looks were equaled by his charm.

They'd filled her with dreams of Hollywood and all the glamorous opportunities awaiting her. That was the reason Angela Rothman had let her friend Julie leave without her. As stupid as it seemed now, she saw her future in those words the dark-haired Cassandra spoke. Even at seventeen, Angela still believed in fairytales and the potential that her chance would someday magically appear.

She remembered laughing. She remembered the tanned, accented young woman buying her a drink. Correction, two drinks. Or was it more? Long Island Iced Tea. She'd never had one before but found it delicious. Her current state being indicative of her overconsumption of the concoction. The clarity seemed to drop off into oblivion after that.

And here she was now, handcuffed in the backseat of a car, shrouded in darkness. Did the brown-eyed driver do this? Whose car was she in? Every question was answered only by another and left her more desperate for answers.

There were a handful of truths she could organize in her mind. One, she had been drinking to the point of blackout. Two, she was in handcuffs. Did she do something wrong? She had been really drunk. Maybe she got into a fight at the bar. Maybe there was a car accident. She began inspecting herself more carefully, looking for clues. No cuts or blood that she could see.

It was the only logical explanation. She'd been stupid and reckless while under the influence, and here she was, stuck in the back of a police car. *My parents are going to kill me. I'll never see the light of day again.* Angela continued to scratch at the edge of a memory she couldn't bring to fruition. Like the flicker of a candle, it was gone. *Why the hell would the cops leave me in the back of a cruiser?* The more her senses returned, she realized this didn't seem like a police car, though. There was no cage separating her from the front seat area. There were no radios squawking.

As if she'd spoken the words aloud, the answer came as the rear passenger door was yanked open. Light shone into the interior compartment of the car, painting the black upholstery a dim yellow. In that moment, she knew she was not in the back of a cruiser.

Angela felt a large hand grip her by the shoulder. The details of the enormous man's face were obscured by the glow of the light behind him. His bald head glimmered as he leaned in.

"Let's go, sweetheart." The big man extracted her from the car and tossed her into a small room. She landed roughly on a stained, uncovered mattress.

The room was chilly compared to the car. She'd never been arrested before, but this wasn't following the script of any tv show or movie she'd ever seen. The lighting conditions were abysmal, the only source coming from the hallway outside. The big man's thick torso blocked most of the yellow hue with his massive shoulders and watermelon-sized head.

"Get your rest. You're gonna need it." He retreated into the hallway.

The door slammed closed and she heard the click of a lock as darkness consumed the surrounding space. Angela wanted to cry, but the dehydration coupled with her mental depletion wouldn't allow for the tears to fall. Instead, she closed her eyes, hoping that when they opened again, this would all be one bad dream. Deep down she was fearful the real nightmare had only just begun.

SIX

THE JINGLE of keys from the other side of the door broke the deafening silence of the room. Without a reference for time, her isolation felt like hours, but it may have been far less. A cold atmosphere seeped from the floors and walls around her. It penetrated the dampness of her jeans, working its way through the fabric and to her bones. Angela was now shivering uncontrollably.

The locking mechanism released, and the metal door creaked loudly as it opened and the yellow light from the hallway filled the room again. She took stock of her surroundings. Not much to see. The room would best be described as a concrete cell. With more of her wits about her, she noticed the only other object in the room aside from the mattress was a plastic blue gallon bucket tucked into the corner opposite her. As embarrassed as she was about urinating in her pants, Angela was grateful they hadn't forced her to relieve herself in the makeshift toilet. With the door open, she could hear an electric hum. The sound reminded her of the oversized freezer her dad kept in his garage.

A man appeared in the doorway. He wasn't the same one who'd shoved her in earlier. This one was young and clean cut, wearing a form-fitting black t-shirt exposing his rigid muscles. He didn't enter the room.

He stood there and said nothing. The smell of his cologne battled against the stink of her confines, penetrating the sourness with a burst of cedarwood and mint. He folded his tightly muscled arms across his chest.

"Hello?" she screamed out.

Nothing in the way of a response came from the silent man in the doorway.

"I want to talk to my lawyer," she yelled. "I know I get a phone call. I know my rights." Angela didn't know her rights nor did she have a lawyer. Her mom had used one seven years ago when she divorced Angela's father, and that was the only lawyer Angela had ever known. And she didn't know him personally. She had to speak to him one time when her parents were deliberating about the custodial arrangement. Angela's only reference came from what she'd seen on tv.

In the dim light, it took about a minute for her eyes to adjust. The fact that she'd abandoned her glasses before going to the bar in an attempt to look more like her sister contributed to the blurriness of her vision. Making out the details of the man's face as best she could, Angela was certain he was not the same one with the beautiful brown eyes and endless smile from the bar.

"Who the hell are you? Where am I?" She asked.

"Shh, pretty girl." In the light, she saw a smirk curl up at the corner of his mouth. He had an accent too, but this was different.

Where the hell am I?

"I want to speak to the police. I want to talk to somebody. Let me... give me my phone." She was desperate. Her voice was ragged. Her teeth chattered as she spoke, a byproduct of the cold and increasing fear. Her heart was beating faster, and she felt the tingle of adrenaline in her fingertips.

She twisted her wrist against the cuff in the hopes she could slip out of it. Angela saw it in an action film once. The hero had broken their own thumb and escaped. She remembered that, even with a broken thumb, the hero was able to fight his way to freedom. She wondered if she could do it. Was she capable of breaking her thumb if needed? Probably not. As much as she'd like to slip off the cuffs and fight her way to freedom, she faced the reality of the situation. Angela knew better. Looking at the muscular man in front of her, who had her by five inches and nearly eighty pounds, it would be impossible. Even if she could free the cuffs, there would be no way she could make it past him and out the door.

And as she debated this impossible conundrum, the bald man entered, eclipsing his counterpart. It was the man with the shiny head and dead, black eyes. He had a thick, black beard that went past his chin, nearly touching his sternum, groomed like a gardener's hedge and glistening in the light from whatever product he used. The heavy-chested man wore a deep-burgundy velour track suit with two white stripes down the side, and a thick, gold chain. He could've passed for an extra on *The Sopranos*. Angela looked around, half expecting to see a camera, as if this were a prank show.

The cartoon mobster almost would have forced a laugh out of the frightened girl had it not been for the eyes. Those cold, black eyes bore into her soul. He met her gaze and then offered a wink.

"Are you going to be a good girl?" The depth of his voice matched the width of his shoulders.

"We've got another girl coming in soon. At least you'll have company. Be a gracious host and tell her how things work around here when she arrives." The bald man rubbed his hands through his thick beard. He then brought his hands together, interlacing his fingers. A rippled popping sound followed as his knuckles cracked loudly.

"Hey, she's a feisty one," the clean-cut man offered. "Even in her condition, she kicked me in the nuts twice when I was trying to get her cuffed. We had to give her a double dose at the first holdover location."

"You got a little fight in you?" The big man asked coyly.

Angela offered her best attempt at a cocky smile. If nothing else, she committed herself to at least giving the impression that this guy couldn't intimidate her, even if deep down, he terrified her. In that moment, she was thankful that she had already released her bladder because if she hadn't, she would be pissing her pants right now. "Take these cuffs off my hands and I'll show you." Her voice betrayed her. The quiver in her throat extended throughout her entire body.

The big man smiled and pulled out a small handcuff key that looked even smaller in his meaty paws.

Angela pushed herself back into the back-left corner of the room as his shadow swallowed the light.

"The Ghost isn't going to like that." The accented voice came from behind the bald man.

"She's a throwaway. She wasn't bought and paid for in advance like the others. You know she doesn't rate tier one status. They don't care what we do with these, as long as they're not broken completely." The bald man laughed.

His laugh scared Angela to her core as he moved toward her.

"Still, we probably shouldn't." The smaller man's plea sounded weak.

"You don't have to do anything except make sure the doors stay shut and that nobody out there hears a thing."

"You're not really going to take her cuffs off, are you?"

"She asked for it." He leaned in close to Angela and pressed his moist forehead against hers. Angela felt as though she was going to vomit. She lashed out with her head. He turned to avoid her assault. Angela's face met the left side of his. His oiled beard softened the blow. She pushed herself forward. Finding his ear, she bit down as hard as she could.

The big man swatted down hard. His forearm caught the side of her head, knocking her into the nearby wall. She tasted his blood as she spat the chunk of flesh from her mouth.

He made no sound. No cry of the pain she'd just inflicted. He leaned in close. His cold dead eyes, darker than her surroundings, stared into her soul. Whatever he saw caused his mouth to twist into a wicked smile. "I knew I'd like you."

The thin man left and locked the door behind him as instructed.

"I like redheads 'cause you're a feisty breed." The big man's fiery breath encircled her in the dark as he spoke. "Fight all you want, sweetheart."

SEVEN

HATCH WALKED through the front entrance of the Hermosa Valley Police Department and was greeted by a fresh-faced patrolman sitting behind a wall of bullet resistant plexiglass. She walked directly to the main desk officer. "I'd like to speak with a detective regarding a missing person," Hatch said.

"Sure thing, let's start by getting your name." His face held a hint of annoyance at her interruption. More so now because he had to work.

Hatch eyed him. In the reflective glare of the picture frame behind the man she noticed he had been hard at work on a digital game of solitaire. She ignored his question about her identity. "I'm just here on a follow-up on the Moss case."

"What agency are you with?"

"Myself. I'm a concerned citizen. I'd like to report an update to the detective assigned follow up on the case. I've just come from the Horton Academy." His face twisted. It was a small twitch, but Hatch noticed. This patrolman knew who and what she was talking about.

"Detective Williamson's handling that case."

"Okay, great. Can I speak to him, then?" Hatch asked.

The man at the desk paused. He looked flustered, but still willing to help. He picked up the phone and punched four digits into the number pad. He cradled the phone against his shoulder and turned away from Hatch.

His voice lowered as he spoke to the detective. "A woman here to see you about the Moss case." He hung up shortly after and turned. Offering a smile more disingenuous than his last. "He'll be down in a moment. You can have a seat over there while you wait. There's a soda machine and restroom if you need."

"Thanks."

Hatch lingered near the bench but didn't sit. She knew all too well the people who frequented the benches of any police department lobby, and they were not ones she wanted to follow. Many of the homeless used police department lobbies as their makeshift shelter, finding refuge in restrooms. Worse in the winter months. In the harsher of climates, they often yearned for arrest just to get a meal and a good night's sleep off the streets.

About seven minutes later, the door beside the main office opened and standing in its wake was a thick-chested man with curly hair the color of molasses wearing a polo-style shirt. His skin was a shade between a deep olive and a soft brown. The Arizona sun agreed with him. Unlike Hatch's pale skin, which could only achieve two colors, white and red. And after the limited exposure in her time in Arizona, she was becoming redder than she liked.

He offered no smile and was not as welcoming as the main desk officer, even if he'd been faking it. This man didn't waste time trying to establish a rapport.

"Can I help you? You told our main desk officer you had information about the Kaitlin Moss case?" He folded his arms across his chest. The sleeves of his shirt exposed his thick forearms. He was not overly muscular. He looked like a power lifter who had maybe surpassed his heyday, but still maintained a light regimen to keep himself fit. The sedentary life of a detective can sometimes wear on the body, and Hatch saw that in the man's rigid exterior.

"Yes," Hatch answered. "Is there a place we can talk in private?" She didn't want to have the conversation in the lobby. More because she wanted the quiet space of an interview room to get as much information about the case from the detective as he expected to get from her.

"Follow me." He unfolded his arms from his chest and swung one out wide, guiding her to the inner sanctum of the small Hermosa Valley Police Department.

They walked down a hallway to the third door on the right. Above it was a placard that read: HVPD Criminal Investigative Service. The door opened to a small space containing four cubicles in a connected row leading to an office at the far end marked "Sergeant". As they passed one of the cubicles, a detective working at his desk looked up briefly as Hatch and Williamson entered and then resumed whatever tedium he was engrossed in. Hatch was happy to see that he wasn't working on a game of solitaire.

"If you like, we could sit in the interview room over here or if you're more comfortable, my desk. It's up to you." He gestured towards a closed room with a single pane of glass in the center of the door shielded by a blind, above it a plaque marked "Interview Room One".

"I'd be more comfortable in the interview room," Hatch said.

He opened the interview room door. "I'm going to grab a cup of coffee from the break room. Would you like one?"

"Sure," Hatch said.

"How do you like it?"

"Sugar and cream would be fine."

"Back in a flash."

He disappeared, leaving Hatch alone in the room. He left the door ajar. She saw the camera in the far-right uppermost corner of the room. It was standard protocol to have a video recording of any interview, whether it was a suspect or witness. It helped to further document the efforts made and sometimes the interviews, when reviewed later, would reveal details not picked up during the actual session.

Hatch looked at the table in front of her. It was cleaner than any interview room she'd ever sat in. She wondered how much experience this department had in handling a kidnapping.

Williamson returned with two cups of coffee in hand. The one in the right he handed to her, and he set his down in front of him. Steam rose from the cups to the cool air-conditioned room. Hatch picked hers up and took a sip. The offering of food and drink was a classic rapport building tactic. He deployed it now in an attempt to soften her. Whatever she had interrupted him doing, he forgot and was now eager to speak with her. She could see he was invested.

He pointed back toward the closed door. "It's not locked. I just like to shut the door for privacy. I need to advise you that there is a recording device on. I forgot to mention it when we first came in. My apologies. But as per policy here at Hermosa Valley, we record everything. Whether it's here in the interview room or out on the street using our body camera system. We are meticulous, and these recordings benefit later review. Do you have a problem with this interview being recorded, Miss...?"

"Nighthawk," Hatch offered.

He eyed her skeptically. "Okay, Miss Nighthawk. I'm Kevin Williamson. I am the detective here in Hermosa Valley and for what it's worth, I've been doing this job for roughly seventeen years."

"Good to know." Hatch didn't offer her first name. And he didn't ask. Not yet anyway.

"Tell me what brings you to our station today and in particular, what information you may have regarding the Kaitlin Moss case?"

"I was at a gas station on the south side of Phoenix. I saw a girl. She looked distraught. At the time I thought nothing of it until right before she went back to the car. Something was off and as she was being put into the backseat, she dropped a small pin."

Williamson jotted a note and then looked up at Hatch. "You said put in the back seat. Was she shoved, forced in any way that you saw?"

"No," Hatch said, "but she looked scared."

"And then what happened?" Williamson asked.

"Like I said, she dropped a small pin. After the car pulled away, I went over and found this." Hatch retrieved the lapel pin from her pocket and then turned it over in her hand, showing him the HA. "It's how I figured out how to go to Horton Academy. I saw this and went there.

When I spoke to the administrative secretary, she provided no information."

"The school already called to let me know you stopped by."

"I understand what you're getting at, but my goal right now is to make sure that this girl is okay. And nobody seems to care."

"I'm sitting here with you right now, aren't I? Trust me, I care. Now, can you start by describing Kaitlin and the people she was with in as much detail as possible?"

Hatch repeated the description she had given the school secretary. Williamson slid out a glossy eight-by-ten photo from within a file folder that he had underneath his notepad.

Smart move, she thought. He waited until she described the girl, rather than showing her the girl first. It was a layer of protection to check the veracity of Hatch's claim. "That's her," she said.

"And how long ago did you see her at this gas station?"

Hatch looked at her watch. "Close to an hour and a half ago."

"Can you give me any details about the vehicle or the people you saw in it?"

Hatch again described the two men. She then pulled out her cellphone and opened to the screenshots she'd taken from the Gas-N-Sip's cameras.

"How'd you get those?"

"The attendant decided it was in his best interest to help a young girl in need."

"Why didn't you call this in? Why go to all the trouble of digging around beforehand?"

Hatch wanted to say *force of habit* but instead offered, "I just wanted to make sure I got the information to the right person. And I'm hoping that person is you."

"I told you I'm thorough. I'm going to take the information you've given me and compare it to what I have so far. I'm going to need you to send me those photos." He slid an embossed business card. "My email's on the bottom."

Williamson pulled out two forms. One had the Hermosa Valley PD logo. The other did not and looked more like a short form legal document.

"Would you be willing to give me a sworn written statement attesting to the information you've provided me here today?"

"I'd prefer to remain anonymous. If that's okay?" Hatch knew it was perfectly fine to receive anonymous tips and information. She hoped her question diminished any suspicion it might rise with Williamson.

"Perfectly fine by me. Less paperwork. But you won't be eligible for this." He smiled, pushing forward the short form. "This is a legal document drafted by the Moss family entitling you to a monetary award, should Kaitlin be found using the information you've just provided."

"I'm not here for a monetary award. I'm here to make sure somebody's out there looking to bring that girl home."

"It's a sizable award." He shrugged and muttered under his coffee breath.

"I don't care how much it's for."

Williamson set his pen atop his note pad. "Well, if there's nothing else, I better get moving on this information. Is there anything else you can remember that may help this investigation?"

"You know what I know. Hopefully, it helps." Hatch stood. "I'll send you those photos."

Williamson escorted Hatch to the door. "Thanks. I appreciate the heads up. But I've got to tell you, everything up to this point is leaning toward the girl running off. Maybe these people you saw her with were some older friends."

"I'd be interested in seeing what her parents would say to that."

"What parents don't know about their kids, especially teenagers, could fill an ocean. I will let 'em know, but I'm confident that she'll turn up in a day or two."

"I'm not."

"While I appreciate your opinion, let's leave the investigation to me. If there's nothing else, I'll see you out."

Hatch walked away with a sense of unease. Williamson didn't impress her. She decided to make one more stop before getting back on the road to California.

EIGHT

HATCH SAT outside the Hermosa Valley Police Department, processing the interview she had just had with Detective Williamson as she emailed the images she'd taken from the Gas-N-Sip. She'd gathered what she needed to follow up on the efforts being made. *Trust and verify.* She had little trust, so the verification was critical if she were to leave Hermosa and get to California.

She considered the reward. Not from the standpoint of regret, but more out of curiosity. The family was offering a sizable reward. Hatch understood affluent families offered monetary compensation in cases like this as a way of motivating citizenry into action. Although it was common practice, that didn't mean there weren't other reasons to do such a thing. And one reason in particular was nagging at her conscience. Was the Moss family offering the money because they had little confidence in the investigative capabilities of their local police force? It was a question Hatch needed an answer to.

It didn't take but a couple of seconds surfing the internet on her cell phone before she found what she was looking for. The Moss family's online presence was a prominent one, especially in the Phoenix area where they were held in royalty-like status. Hatch scrolled through pictures of their home in Hermosa Estates, the most exclusive of neighborhoods, set against the backdrop of Camelback Mountain. The low-end prices of the houses were two to three million dollars.

Kaitlin Moss had a Facebook profile set to private, but Hatch could see the profile picture was a family portrait that included her mother and father. Hatch stared at the girl in the picture. She looked happy, even if the photo was staged. Hatch remembered seeing her at the gas station. If Hatch had reacted when she first saw her then she'd be back with her family right now. Hesitation had played a part in derailing her life before. She wasn't about to let it happen again. The guilt she'd feel if anything happened to the teenager would be unbearable.

After digging around and gathering information, it wasn't long before she had a physical address for the family's palatial home. Mapping it on her phone, she realized it was less than twenty minutes away from her current location.

The air conditioning was working overtime. After a few minutes of driving, the tingling remnants of the Arizona sun subsided as she drove toward the exclusive neighborhood. Hatch pulled down the Moss' street. She was awestruck at the size of the mansions lining both sides of the wide roadway. Each with their own high walls and landscaping designed to provide privacy while maintaining aesthetics. The phrase keeping up with the Joneses had reached pinnacle proportions as each house she passed was larger and more audacious than the previous. At the end of the street was the largest of them all. The digital pushpin on her map indicated it belonged to the Moss family.

Hatch put her bias toward the super-rich aside. She came to help a family find their daughter. Cases like that bypassed any boundaries created by wealth and circumstance, and she expected the family inside would be as worried as anybody else.

Hatch pulled up to a gated entrance, a black, wrought-iron fence encased in a cherry colored wood set in a beige stucco wall, decorated with hand-painted tiles. The gate closed with an arched center. Hearty trees stretched their branches out, creating a canopy. Hatch caught a glimpse of herself in the side mirror as she exited the vehicle. She couldn't feel more out of place in her t-shirt and jeans. On more than one occasion during her early years as an MP, Hatch had gone to a two-star general's house on a domestic disturbance. At the time, that house seemed enormous. But now, standing in the shade of the Catclaw Acacia trees outside the Moss estate, the general's house seemed more like a gardener's shed.

There was a call box on the right. The metal face of the keypad display was hidden inside a decorative lacquered wooden case. In the few seconds Hatch took to open it, her mind flooded with doubt. She prided herself on her level of unparalleled confidence but in the short interim since leaving Hawk's Landing and entering uncharted territory, she questioned herself more frequently.

Detective Williamson was working the case and was now armed with the information she'd provided. Yet here she was, standing outside the gates of the missing girl's massive home. She asked herself an important question. *Why?* Clarity came from her answer: *help good people and punish those who hurt others.*

She lifted the latch, accessed the box's interface, and pressed the only button, marked Guard House.

"Moss residence. Can I help you?" a gruff, throaty voice said through the intercom's speaker system. Hatch envisioned a large man behind that voice.

"I'm here to speak with Mr. and Mrs. Moss," Hatch sounded as if she had an appointment, delivering her request with an air of confidence.

"I'm sorry, but the Moss family is unavailable right now. Who may I ask is calling?"

"My name is Daphne Nighthawk and I have information regarding their daughter Kaitlin."

There was a metallic click followed by silence. Hatch assumed the security guard was relaying the information to his employer. Less than a minute later, the voice came back. "Please forward any information you have to the Hermosa Valley Police Department. The Moss family appreciates your interest and support in helping find their daughter, but they cannot entertain anyone at this time. The family is under a great deal of stress and would like to be left alone."

"I've already talked to the police department," Hatch said.

"Well, then you've done your job and the Moss family appreciates it. Should the information provided result in the location and/or return of their daughter, compensation will be awarded." He said the last part in a rehearsed sing-song voice, and Hatch envisioned the guard rolling his eyes. "Have a good day," he offered flatly before clicking off.

Hatch pressed the button again.

"Seems like you just don't get it." This time his voice was even more gruff than before. Whatever professionalism he'd attempted to convey the first go round had dissipated into the oppressive air.

"It's imperative that I speak with either Mr. or Mrs. Moss immediately. Their daughter's safety... her life depends on it."

"I don't know how to make this any clearer to you, lady." There was no hiding the frustration in his voice. "The Moss family does not want to be disturbed. If you have information like you say you do and you've already forwarded it to the police department, then you've done your due diligence. The detective in charge is working closely with the Moss family in bringing this situation to resolution."

"I understand their need for privacy, but what I have to tell them won't take long and if—"

"You are currently standing on private property," the guard interrupted. "By Arizona law, I'm authorized to physically remove you from the property should you remain after being advised to leave." His words came through a clenched jaw. "I'm advising you that, as of right now, you are trespassing. You're to leave the property immediately."

Hatch thought for a moment about this advice being delivered through the small box. Leaving meant that everything she had told Detective Williamson would rest solely in his hands. She worried that the information she had relayed had either fallen on deaf ears or would not be pursued to its end. Pressure from the Moss family would be critical in making the needed impact with the investigators. A brief conversation with the parents of the missing girl would give Hatch a smidgen of peace for her restless mind. The squeaky wheel gets the oil, and Hatch wanted to ensure Detective Williamson heard the squeak. A parent who continually pressed law enforcement for an answer usually got one, but whether the answer turned out to be what they wanted was a different story.

Hatch rooted herself in her stance and peered through the iron bars at the small adobe shed set back from the gate. The darkened windows of the guard house made it near impossible for Hatch to see inside. The position of the guard house was strategic. Set ten feet from the gate, the guard inside had time to react if anyone breached the perimeter. Beyond the guard shed's walls, the Moss house sat an additional fifty feet from the gate. Hatch imagined there were other security personnel inside.

She watched and waited. A moment later, the door to the guard house opened, and she quickly realized that the voice she'd heard through the call box matched perfectly to the body of the angry-eyed man storming her way.

He was a large man between six-foot-one and six-foot-three, a few inches taller than Hatch. From the muscles pressing against the slick fabric of the designer suit, he weighed around two-hundred-and-thirty pounds. She figured most of his body mass was comprised of muscle.

The cut of the suit looked professionally tailored. Not surprising, given his employer. The suit's material shimmered in the Arizona sun. He wore a collared shirt with no tie. By the time he crossed the distance and stood in front of Hatch, beads of sweat had already formed on his brow.

Hatch couldn't imagine this being a busy job for the guard. Her interruption had upset him in whatever his daily routine was, not unlike the solitaire playing main desk officer or the nonchalant detective. For a half-a-second, Hatch felt as though someone trapped her in an episode of the Twilight zone where everybody she had encountered seemed too busy to help this missing girl. The more likely reality was that her tenacity was rarely matched.

The guard was now standing only a few inches away with the gate being their only barrier. He stared at her for a moment, sizing her up. He struck a Superman pose, opening into a wide stance and placing his hands on his hips. It was obvious that in the past he'd used his impressive size to intimidate people like a bouncer at a bar. He was using it now to no effect. Hatch stood her ground and met his gaze.

"Lady, I don't know what your problem is, but the Moss family doesn't want you here. And I'm going to make it real simple for you." He thumbed back towards the house. "You see the size of that? They pay me good money to keep crazy people from coming on their property. I'm very good at keeping crazy out of this house. So, do me a favor and make it easy on yourself. Get in your little car and drive away. The family does not want to be disturbed."

Hatch softened her tone. Meeting aggression with aggression wasn't always the answer. Redirection had a purpose, and she figured she'd give it a shot here. "Listen, I don't want any trouble. All I want is to speak with either Mr. or Mrs. Moss. They need to hear what I have to say. What they decide to do with it after that point will be solely on them. Yes, I told the police department, but I don't know that they're doing an adequate job. And the information I have is pressing." Hatch watched him shake his head as she spoke, bringing her annoyance to a boil. "Every minute I stand here wasting time talking with you is time that could be put to good use in possibly finding their daughter. So how about you get your overgrown gym muscles out of the way and let me in? Or have Mrs. Moss or her husband come down to the gate so I can speak to them."

"They're not here," he said, flustered.

"That's not what you said before," Hatch responded. "You said they were not taking visitors at this time. That means somebody's home and they don't want to be disturbed. Now you're telling me they're not home."

"It doesn't matter what I said. It's time for you to go."

Movement caught Hatch's eye in a second-floor window of the home behind the guard. Hatch cast a quick glance in that direction and for a split second thought she was looking at the missing girl. Looking at Kaitlin Moss. Blonde hair, tan skin. Hatch's eyes focused and she noticed the face in the window was older. Their eyes met and Hatch could tell the woman was completely and wholly distraught. An instant later, she disappeared.

Hatch turned her attention back to the guard. "I know they're home."

"I'm done listening to you, lady. I'm gonna give you the option I reserve for my favorite unwanted visitors. Easy way or hard way. What's it going to be?"

Hatch's mood soured. She looked back at her car, then at the guard who'd just threatened her. Her arms dangled loosely by her side, but tension rose in her spine. "I'd really prefer the easy way. I'm not looking for trouble, but I'm not leaving until I speak to somebody."

"Sounds like you chose the hard way," he said. Hatch caught a slight smile curl up around the corner of his mouth.

He then reached forward and manually released the gate's lock. He seemed to take pleasure in this slow methodical movement as if unlocking the gate was going to intimidate her and she'd turn tail and run back to her car. She offered him no such satisfaction and stepped forward with her left foot, planting the weight on her back foot as she prepared for his next move. The time for talk was over and Hatch was now evaluating the circumstance playing out before her.

He yanked back the gate, just enough so he could slip through. He was taking the precaution so as not to give her any opportunity to shoot inside. The guard stepped through the opening. While his body was halfway between the open gate, Hatch snatched out with both hands. She grabbed him by his exposed right shoulder and pulled hard, slamming him face forward into the metal of the gate. The large guard's nose crashed into the hard iron.

While the guard reeled, she shot out her left hand and grabbed the open end of the gate. She pulled it toward her, slamming it into the back of his head. The two concussive forces sent the man backwards, dazed and staggering. Both his hands were now cupping his nose as blood poured from his nostrils.

He looked at Hatch through his watering eyes. His face was red with rage, almost matching the color of the blood. The guard balled his fist and lunged forward, but Hatch was already in motion. She struck out with her right elbow, slamming it into the side of his neck. Staggered and off balance, the guard wobbled as Hatch hooked his ankle with hers and yanked it back. The combination of strike plus sweep worked to topple the top-heavy guard. He was now flat on his back and Hatch stood over him.

"You crazy bitch." He spat blood and brought himself to a seated position. He pulled a pistol as he stood.

Hatch considered taking the weapon from the guard, but things had already escalated to a point of limited return. She stepped back. Any chance she had of helping the girl would go up in smoke if she ended up locked in Hermosa Valley PD. She was dizzy from this current setback. Standing in the driveway of the biggest house she'd ever seen after bludgeoning a security guard who worked for the family she was trying to help didn't bode well. How quickly things had gotten out of hand. First things first, she needed to address the gun pointed at her head. Although Hatch was confident the guard wouldn't shoot, her hands went up.

"Listen, I wasn't kidding. What I have to say is important." She took two steps back, now losing her foothold on the ground. She wanted to make a mad dash for the front door but knew the guard would then be more inclined to fire his gun. He would justify it as protecting the family from a lunatic. She assumed there were video cameras all around the grounds of the estate. He wouldn't shoot unless she forced his hand. She could see the hatred in his eyes and the embarrassment at being bested by a smaller female. It had probably never happened to him and would probably not happen again. This life lesson was a one-time gift, but the lesson was over. With everything that had transpired, Hatch realized she had reached a stalemate.

"Please, tell the family to call the police department. I gave Detective Williamson the information. It's imperative. Their daughter is alive. Their daughter is in trouble and I can help." She still had her hands raised.

"Get the hell out of here before I shoot you dead." He spat the words, staining the paved stones with his blood. He held the weapon, shaking, aiming at her center of mass. Blood continued to flow from his nose. He used the sleeve of his fancy suit to wipe it.

"I'm leaving now. Tell them what I said." Hatch walked backwards towards her car, never breaking her stare from the gunman. She knew the likelihood of the bodyguard relaying her message was close to zero, but Hatch banked on the fact the mother had witnessed the exchange and would question what happened. Hatch's desperate act might have served its purpose after all.

Hatch got into her car. The air conditioning was still running. She looked in the rearview mirror. Not one bead of sweat had formed.

As Hatch drove away, she realized there was another way of ensuring her message was received.

NINE

"I DON'T LIKE COMPLICATIONS," Mr. Carmen stated. "Who is she?"

"I don't know. Good Samaritan, I guess. She saw the package at the gas station and has been digging on her own. She's already spoken to the police, and I just got word she paid a visit to the parents' home. She beat up their gate security officer."

"Is she going to be an issue?"

"Not as far as I'm concerned."

"Contain the problem," Mr. Carmen said.

Carmen's marching orders were clear, though the execution of such tasking had always been left up to his discretion on how to best handle it. He was a trusted member of the organization and had his role as the Arizona branch manager established early on. The network's expansive reach required the organizational structure to be very well-defined, like a multi-state chain store. Demand was high for the product they delivered, and the pay was commensurate with the duties he was assigned.

"I have that worked out. It's just going to take a little finesse to ensure it's done in a way that won't lead back to us." It wasn't an ideal situation. With a random do-gooder running around stirring things up, he couldn't just put a bullet in her head. It would draw too much heat. But he had put a contingent in place at the onset of this delivery. This package was the most lucrative to date and he'd taken the time to plan for every possible eventuality. While this nosy woman's antics warranted concern, it was manageable. That's one of the reasons they called him Ghost. He could make people disappear. She would be no different.

"This is a big haul. Do you understand?" Mr. Carmen continued. "The potential for exposure is high with this one. This could change things for the business if it goes through without a hitch. That, coupled with the extra packages to accompany this delivery, leaves us little wiggle room for error. You need to make sure things go as smooth as possible; we don't need any additional attention drawn to us. Am I making myself clear?"

"Crystal. No need to worry, sir." It had been a while since he'd had to call somebody sir, but this man warranted it, not only by the money he paid but by the power he wielded. Mr. Carmen was somebody to keep in good graces with. The short-term benefits of his newfound job had drastically changed his lifestyle over the last few years. It had given him the access to a level of monetary wealth he never dreamed possible. But as with many high-paying jobs, this one didn't have a retirement benefit. There was no 401k package in the world of human trafficking. And the severance package, should termination be deemed necessary, came in the form of a coffin. Ghost had been responsible for removing employees in the past and planned to avoid making it on that list.

In the few years he'd been working for the company, Ghost witnessed top-level guys in the organization take an "early retirement." This was a joke that garnered a few laughs from the men in his employ. Retirement came in the form of a bullet to the back of the head; one they never saw coming. Many of those bullets came from Ghost himself. This made him extra cautious, almost to a point of hypervigilance. Aware that at any moment he could shift from his current golden boy status to being top on the removal list.

Ghost liked where he was. He wanted it to stay like this for as long as he could. He'd been trying to work out an exit strategy and had started banking his money in offshore accounts. The accumulating wealth was nearing the number he'd come up with that would allow him to disappear off the face of the earth forever. He was getting close to that magic number. Everybody had a number, and Ghost's was high. If attained, it would secure a level of financial wealth and comfort capable of carrying him all the way to his grave.

He figured he was one year from hitting his magic number, based on the earnings he'd made over the last few years. A year ago, he started shuffling the money to an account that couldn't be traced. He had several IDs that had been forged by his employer, so his new identity was set: fingerprints, birth certificate, license and passport, the works. It was all prepared when the time came. Or if he fell out of favor with Mr. Carmen. He knew how best to avoid that. Listening to his employer now and the tension and anger that was barely veiled behind the man's voice, Ghost knew that he must eliminate this new threat.

"Do you have a name on her, a background, anything?"

"She signed in at the school as Daphne Nighthawk. I've run the name through my sources and haven't found anything. At least nothing local. I'll keep digging. It's what I do best. If there's a crumb to find, I'll find it."

"Is she using a fake name?" Mr. Carmen asked.

"Maybe. Who knows? But I'm telling you, it won't matter in a couple hours." Ghost didn't elaborate. "But I'd like to find out as much as I can before she's removed, so I can ensure you nobody else will be following in her footsteps and raising any additional red flags."

"Well, without knowing her background or why she's prying so deeply, we're going to have to step up our efforts and make sure she doesn't dig any further."

"You trust me to handle this, right?" There was a silence. In the absence of words came concern.

"I do."

"And you know that when I handle it, there'll be no trace of her. I don't want to underestimate her, and I have a plan in place for such a situation."

"I'm giving you a short leash. Know that if anything happens to the packages, if they're compromised in any way, you'll be joining Ms. Nighthawk."

"You won't regret it." Ghost didn't like the comparison of him to a dog. Because a dog is exactly how Mr. Carmen saw him. But there it was, unveiled and exposed. The threat to him was clear. Handle this one wrong and it would be the last operation he'd ever be involved with. A year from retirement suddenly seemed far away. He'd always been confident when it came to handling the business end. He'd done it in the past, he'd do it again now. When it was all said and done, his employer would see his ability to handle the unforeseen and be reaffirmed in his decision to bring him into the fold. He resolved how the woman would die. And from that death, Ghost would remain Mr. Carmen's right-hand man.

Throughout his life, he'd been tested on his ability to do the unthinkable. With each new task, he was forced to prove himself again and again. He would be foolish to think this one didn't matter the most. His life depended on it.

Ghost had a plan. He learned long ago if you fail to plan, then you plan to fail. Although life had thrown him a few curve balls, as it did everyone, failure had never been an option for him in his prior career path, nor the one that had chosen him now.

He'd made more this year than he'd made in the ten years he served his previous employer. He was grateful for the cash but knew it came at a heavy cost. Ghost had long ago sold his soul and wasn't holding out any hope that the pearly gates would be open to the likes of him. In accepting who he was and accepting his fate, he embraced the mortality of his life. Being close to death gave him perspective. The money would enable him to have his own piece of heaven here on earth.

He was in the final phase of closing on a small bungalow on an island far from the Arizona valley. This island was where his new identity would take shape, and nobody would be able to track him down. Four months to go and the bungalow would be his. Eight more after that, he would be sipping rum, watching the waves roll in.

The world around him was as complicated as a Rubik's Cube. Ghost hoped he had better luck in life than he did twisting that colorful block. In his youth, he had only managed to get two sides completed, and it always frustrated him. He hoped in life that he could master all six. Right now, he was closing in on that. He just had to ensure that Daphne Nighthawk didn't wreck his plans. And in doing so, didn't remove his favor with his employer. When this was all said and done and the packages were delivered, Ms. Nighthawk would be dead.

He understood why this one was more complicated. The high value package that was being delivered had come at great cost. As with any substantial reward, it came at an equally significant risk. The money that had already changed hands for the girl was beyond what he'd ever seen any prize go for in his years of service. And that was just the down payment. The buyer would release the second installment of equal value upon receipt of the Moss girl. She was akin to the white whale in Moby Dick. Ghost guessed that made him *Queequeg*. He hoped he didn't go down with the ship as Herman Melville's tale depicted in his classic novel. He wanted to bring this whale in. No chance a random outsider would sink his opportunity.

There might be a sizable bonus that could be enough to expedite his retirement. Bonuses were inconsistently dished out. But the extra precautions and layered approach to this operation would please his employer enough to earn a little extra. Ghost knew it all hinged on how cleanly he disposed of this Daphne Nighthawk.

"If this one goes off without a hitch, there might be extra in it for you," Mr. Carmen said.

Like a dog smelling food in his dish, Ghost salivated. Money got his blood pumping. His insatiable quest to fill his cup until it ran over became an obsessive compulsion that only worsened with each dollar added to his surplus pile. It consumed him. It was the last thing he thought of before he went to bed and the first thing when he woke up.

He'd never had much growing up. His early years of life he had to fight for scraps as he bounced around the foster system. It wasn't until he found his calling did his desire recede. It was a long time until the longing returned. When he'd been exposed to real power and the real money backing it, Ghost's hunger for it became insatiable. Then the opportunity presented, and he leapt at it.

Ghost was now as painfully tied to his bank account's balance as Gollum was the ring. The power of it called out to him. It forced him to do things he would've never deemed possible. He took solace in the money. It was antiseptic for his wounded soul at the tasks he was called to perform. Over time, the doing of evil became easier, like weight gain. Each awful order carried out, even though worse than its predecessor, led to the point where taking a human life had zero emotional cost. In fact, he'd come to enjoy that aspect. The act itself created its own strange emotional reward system.

He wanted to see a shrink. Ghost felt his mind should be studied by experts in the world of psychology. He wasn't always this person. It was as if he'd lived two lives. At times, he had trouble even remembering anything significant from his former self. Two souls occupied his body. The darker, more sinister one had taken the reins, guiding him the last few years.

He'd come up with a thousand different ways to justify his actions, but in the end, it came down to one simple thing. Money, and the need for it.

"Don't worry about a thing. She'll be dead by dawn." Ghost knew the same fate would be true of him if he failed.

TEN

HATCH IDLED in the Ford as she waited outside of the road to Hermosa Estates, where more normal sized houses populated her field of vision. She was within a block of the street to Kaitlin Moss's home. She'd been sitting in this same spot for an hour. During the first fifteen minutes, she'd watched carefully for any sign that law enforcement had been notified about the bludgeoned guard. There was none.

Hatch continued to wait, watching for somebody else. Just passing the hour mark, she observed a powder blue Mercedes S-class convertible approach the stop light at the intersection. In the driver's seat was the same blonde-haired woman she'd seen in the window when confronting the guard, Willow Moss.

At a closer range, Hatch could see the lines of worry etched deeply into the contours of her smooth face. She looked around, her head skittishly checking her surroundings. Hatch surmised the strain of the situation was too much. Or maybe seeing the bloody guard had done more to shock her than Hatch initially intended. Willow Moss was frazzled as she turned left.

Hatch let a few cars pass and slipped into the light flow of traffic. She wasn't sure if Willow would recognize her, but she didn't want to chance it. She didn't want to spook Willow any further. Hatch's purpose and intention was clear. Contacting Kaitlin's mother was her best hope of accomplishing that.

Every turn Willow made, Hatch kept a few cars between them. She kept the Mercedes in sight by adjusting her vehicle position within its lane of travel based on Willow's driving, Hatch concluded the mother of the missing girl had no idea she was being followed. Hatch had done surveillance and countersurveillance. She'd fancied herself adept at maneuvering herself without detection, although this circumstance didn't warrant that level of skill.

Willow pulled into an angled spot along a strip of fancy shops and restaurants and figured this must be Phoenix's version of Rodeo Drive. Hatch had never been one for materialism and being here now only further supported her opinion.

Hatch pulled the Focus into a parking space, four away from where Willow had parked. She caught a couple glances of Willow. She was out of her element. A strange sensation for Hatch, a woman who would be more comfortable in the jungles of Africa fighting alongside Jabari and his team. To her, the battlefield was more comforting than sitting here among the wealthy.

She pulled out her cell phone and held it to her ear, pretending to be engaged in a conversation as she watched Willow out of the corner of her eye. She wished now, after seeing the way the people around her looked, that she had put on nicer clothes than the lightweight t-shirt and jeans that she was wearing. What nagged her more was the looks her damaged skin would draw amidst all the perfect, sun-kissed people. She hated herself for not being able to dismiss the looks she garnered when people first saw her.

Hatch felt she'd stick out like a sore thumb, but inside the car, no one took notice of her. She dipped her body just a little, lowering her profile, shrinking herself. Her height always got a couple looks, but it was the scarred arm that earned her the guaranteed double takes. And Willow had taken a careful look at her when she had peered out the window of her home.

Willow exited her Mercedes. The alarm chirped as she walked toward the long line of stores. She was wearing a silk summer dress. Her body was toned, bronzed, like that of Kaitlin's. She looked wiry, strong, and healthy. Hatch surmised Willow engaged in recreational physical training. From the elongated, toned muscles, she guessed yoga was her means to fitness. Or running. Maybe the two had more in common than Hatch realized.

Willow carried a mid-sized box and walked inside a boutique called Dream Catcher. Hatch waited for five minutes, still using the phone against her ear as she sat. She didn't want to immediately follow the distraught mother inside. She hadn't seen any bodyguards but wanted to make sure no other car contained unwanted eyes. Satisfied the coast was clear, she turned the ignition off. The air conditioning, which had been working overtime against the heat, sputtered slightly before coming to a complete stop and Hatch exited.

She paused to look at herself in the reflection of the front door's mirrored glass. The woman staring back at her was unforgiving. Her pale skin gave her a ghostlike appearance when held in contrast to the others moving about her. Hatch's raised scar tissue twisted around her arm like the thorny branch of a rose bush with the tattoo adding to it. Add in her non-designer apparel, and Hatch understood why her mere presence caused more than a few people to take a second glance. She didn't like it, but she ignored it just the same.

The hand painted sign above the door had an oversized version of a Native American talisman, woven to ward off bad dreams and nightmares. Hatch jokingly entertained the idea that entering the store would remove the nightmare that was her life, like the woven hoop was designed to do. She laughed at herself for the foolish mental diversion as she walked inside.

The store was quiet, except for the low hum of rhythmic soothing music playing in the backdrop. There was the smell of freshly steeped tea and honey. In the back near the checkout was a station for people to get refreshments while they shopped. A few tables were set in the back.

Presumably, rich people needed to rest. Spending all that money exhausted them.

The box Willow had carried into the store was now on the counter. Beside it was a beautiful, brightly colored, handmade planter. The lanky man behind the counter grinned as he inspected it.

Why would someone as rich as Willow Moss be selling to a boutique? Hatch couldn't hear the exchange as she stood by a rack of clothes near the entrance. Willow then turned and made eye contact with Hatch for a moment, then she turned back to the salesperson and said something out of earshot. Hatch eyed the door and considered making a hasty departure but decided against it as Willow walked in her direction.

Willow went to a nearby rack of clothes and began thumbing through a smattering of airy dresses. Her hands trembled. Hatch came up beside her and pretended to be interested in the selection.

"Can't talk here," Willow whispered. "I'm going to buy a dress and then I'm going to get back in my car and drive. Follow me and make sure you're not followed."

Hatch nodded. She let go of the tag she was holding, releasing the lightweight dress, then left the store.

The minutes dragged on while Hatch waited for Willow. Every person who walked by, or car that passed, were on Hatch's radar. Willow's comment had Hatch concerned but after vigilantly scanning the area, nobody stood out from the flow.

After a while, Willow exited the store with a small shopping bag. She slipped into her car and pulled out of her parking spot. Again, Hatch followed, now unconcealed from the distraught mother's rearview as they drove away.

ELEVEN

ON THE DRIVE from Hermosa Valley, Willow stayed off the interstate, navigating backroads until the two women came to a lot that bordered a park extending across a three-block swath of North 34 Avenue in the heart of central Phoenix. It was a total departure from the world they'd just left a mere half an hour ago.

Willow pulled her Mercedes into an open spot near a red and green canopied PlayScape. There was a tall palm tree and an ironwood tree, both adjacent to the spot and providing a small amount of shade. Unlike the cluster of well-maintained trees of the Valley, this area looked more like a desert sandlot. Hatch parked six spots from Willow's car.

It was clear they'd left the affluence of Hermosa crossing over the invisible border, and Hatch felt a thousand times more comfortable in her current surroundings.

Willow looked around at the sparse parking lot and abandoned field of sunburnt grass before stepping out in the Arizona heat. She walked over to a covered patio that shaded a poured concrete slab with a faded green thermoplastic picnic table and took up a seat. Willow sat with her back straight and her hands folded atop her lap. There was a regal air to her posture, but her face was gentle and welcoming. She looked as out of place in this setting as Hatch was in Willow's neighborhood.

A pair of swings creaked in the warm breeze, calling out to the children who were nowhere in sight. In the distance, Hatch saw a girl about Daphne's age rise and fall on a seesaw with an older boy on the other end. She heard a giggle and the sound soured in her ears. Hatch knew the pain of leaving Daphne and Jake behind and couldn't fathom what Willow must be going through. Looking across at the poise in the distraught mother's face, Hatch saw strength as she sat down across from Willow.

"First off, let me start by saying, I've already dialed 911 on my phone. All I have to do is hit the call button."

Hatch looked down at Willow's hands. Her thumb hovered above the green call icon on her cell phone's screen. It trembled.

"You won't need that." Hatch placed her hands on the table. "I just want to talk to you. I'm here to help."

"I'm hoping it's about my daughter." Willow's voice cracked as she fought back tears and set aside the phone.

"It is. I've already told the police, but—"

"Let me guess..." Willow rolled her eyes. "Williamson?"

Hatch nodded.

"He's about as useless as they come, but he's a friend of the family, so my husband trusts him."

"And you don't?"

"Not as far as I could throw him. My husband grew up with him. They're old high school football buddies." She fiddled with the enormous diamond set in her wedding ring. "Obviously, life took them down different paths, but I didn't come from money."

"What have they done so far with the investigation?"

"Not much," Willow said. "Every time my husband gets an update, he just tells me they're working on it. He doesn't let me speak with Williamson."

"Doesn't let you?" Hatch could see Willow was crumbling.

"Kyle's very controlling."

Hatch didn't press further. Not that she didn't want to, but her focus was on relaying the information about her daughter.

"Did your husband tell you I saw her?"

"My Kaitlin?" Willows eyes widened and tears welled up in the outer corners. "You saw my baby girl?"

Williamson hadn't even updated the family! Hatch fumed. *Or he had, and Willow's husband held it back from her.*

"I saw her earlier this morning at a gas station close to here." Hatch saw Willow ready to sprint to her car and drive there now, as if catching the remote tendril of her daughter's trail would bring her closer to her. "The information I'm going to tell you should have been relayed to you by now. That it didn't is concerning, but right now I need to get you caught up. When I saw Kaitlin, she was in a vehicle with two older men."

"Oh God!" Willow shrieked.

Hatch pulled out her cell phone and scrolled through the images she'd taken from the gas station's security camera. Willow gasped at the sight of Kaitlin. Her hand reached out as if she could grab her.

"Have you ever seen either of these men before?"

Willow shook her head, causing her tears to zigzag on her cheek.

"I gave all of this to Williamson before coming to your house."

"Why did you come to my house after talking to the police?"

"I didn't like the lack of urgency with which Williamson took the information. I felt it best I spoke to you directly. Figured you could motivate him to do his job better than I could."

"Thank you." Willow wiped at her eyes, smearing her makeup, making her look as though she were returning from a long night of partying. "If you hadn't come to me who knows how long it would've taken before I found out. I told my husband Kevin Williamson was a lazy, good for nothin' bastard." Willow spat the words while dropping her more refined speech, exposing to Hatch another layer of herself. "Sorry, I come back here, and I don't feel the need to put on airs."

"You lived here?" Hatch asked in a non-judgmental tone, realizing the millionaire's wife had grown up on the poor side of town.

"Grew up in that house right behind you." Willow pointed to a rundown ranch-styled home on the other side of the street. The chain-link fence gate looked nothing like the one of her current estate. It was dented, half of it laying on the patchy lawn littered with beer cans. "Didn't look much better when I lived there. Long time ago but feels like yesterday."

Hatch understood the sentiment.

"I come here for perspective sometimes." She looked past Hatch to the front door of her childhood home. "Like the fact that my jerk of a husband didn't tell me our daughter was in trouble. And that his goon stopped you from delivering me the message."

"Sorry about beating up your guard," Hatch said.

"Teddy."

Teddy?

Fitting for a man the size of a bear, yet he didn't seem so cuddly.

"Teddy is a jerk," Willow said flatly. "Again, hired by my husband. Rarely does he take orders from me. Do you know what he told me? He said you were a crazy person trying to take credit for finding her. He told my husband the same thing."

"And he believed it?"

"He believes what Teddy said."

"Do you?"

"Think you're a crazy woman looking for a reward? I hope I'm not wrong in saying this, but no, I don't think you're crazy." She tried to smile but failed. "I would tell Kyle what you told me, but it wouldn't matter. He doesn't listen to me. Never has. Why would he start now?"

Hatch felt for this mother. Her daughter was missing, and her husband was botching any chance of recovery by trusting his childhood friends and moronic guards. Was this all to protect his image? She didn't have much of a mental repository from which to draw any experience investigating crimes against the ultrarich.

Hatch sensed that Willow suffered abuse at the hands of Kyle. Whether it was physical or psychological, there was at least one layer.

"Tell me about Kaitlin. From when you saw her?" Willow's hands continued to tremble.

Hatch reached over and settled her hand on Willow's. The exposed scar drew the mother's eye as Hatch recounted the event. When she finished, Willow asked, "How do you know so much about this stuff? Are you a cop?"

"Yes, a long time ago."

Willow didn't press for an explanation, and Hatch didn't offer one. She picked up Hatch's phone and zoomed in on the picture of her daughter before the girl disappeared into the SUV. A tear fell from Willow's face and dropped onto the phone's screen. Once the first tear fell, the floodgates opened wide, and she sobbed uncontrollably. Hatch sat by and allowed the mother to grieve. The pain was palpable and understandable. Willow's breathing changed and was nearing a point of a hyperventilation.

"Breathe," Hatch said. "Take a deep, long inhale and hold it for a four count before releasing. I'll do it with you." She coached Willow through. She had figured out the best way to get the mind under control during emotional stress was to oxygenate the brain. It was the ultimate tool in resetting the mind. Operators, like Hatch, had been using this technique since the dawn of war. They called it box breathing: inhale four seconds, hold four seconds, exhale four seconds, wait four seconds. It had never failed Hatch when she needed to eliminate distractions and reduce anxiety.

Willow followed Hatch's lead, and within a minute she was calm again. Wiping the tears from her face, she offered an apologetic look. "I'm sorry," her voice cracked for a second time.

"Don't be. Can you tell me a little about your daughter? To help me find her?"

"You'd be willing to do that? Help me find her?" Willow asked, shock replacing the sorrow of the previous moment. "Why? Who... who are you?"

Hatch offered a gentle smile. "She seems like a good person. You do, too. And good people need somebody willing to look out for them. And this isn't a typical runaway case. Figured reaching out to you was the least

I could do. Now I need to do more." She steeled her expression and tightened her grip on the woman's hand. "I *have* to do more."

"I've already hired somebody to look into it." Willow's voice regained its strength. "Well, *I* didn't, my husband did. He did it just to shut me up so I wouldn't keep complaining about Williamson and the investigation."

"A private detective?" Hatch asked.

"Yes. His name is Colton Gibbons. I wasn't sure about him at first, but Kyle swore to me he was reputable."

"Do you have his contact information? I'd like to reach out if that's okay with you?"

"That'd be fine by me." Willow was quiet for a moment. Her eyes settled back on the busted fence of her old home. "He wasn't always like this. Or maybe I was just blinded by the world he introduced me to. I mean, look around and you can see how far I've come."

"Wealth doesn't always equal happiness." Hatch felt silly espousing wisdom she couldn't validate. She'd never known wealth or moved in circles of people who did. So, the vapid message held no value.

"I know that. At least I do now. But fifteen years ago, I was a different person."

Hatch remembered who she was fifteen years ago, too. A young girl entering womanhood through a baptism of fire courtesy of the United States Army. The years in between had forever changed her. On this front, Hatch understood. "I get it. Truly, I do."

"I was young and dumb. Kaitlin was two. Kyle gave me—and more importantly Kaitlin—a better chance at life. It's all a parent cares about. Back then, Kyle was decent enough." Willow looked down at the cracked concrete beneath her five hundred-dollar sandals. "Things changed. I've been trying to make my break. I was going to wait until Kaitlin finished school. But I have a plan."

"I'm not judging you. It takes as much courage to walk away as it does to stay." Hatch referenced her decision to leave the military. It was the longest love-hate relationship of her life.

"That's what you saw me doing at the boutique. When Kyle and I were first dating, he took me to the City of Puebla in Mexico. A beautiful place. I fell in love with Talavera Pottery. I spent time learning the art form while we visited. When we returned, Kyle gave me my own studio and kiln. He even flew in a master artisan to privately teach me."

Hatch's eyes widened a bit, trying to fathom a lifestyle where this kind of thing was commonplace.

"Like I said that kindness vanished some time ago. But I've been making Talavera pots ever since. Dream Catcher is one of a handful of stores that sells my artwork on consignment. I've saved every penny I've made over the last ten years hoping when the time comes to leave him, I'll have enough to jumpstart my next life. My new life." Willow absently brushed back her blonde hair from her face, tucking it behind her ears. Her eyes watered again. "*Our* new life."

"What about the private detective?" Hatch redirected Willow's focus to the investigation.

"He's okay, I guess. He was running the leads gathered from the police investigation. He keeps me informed, but everybody he's talked to has said the same thing. A couple of students who last saw her said she got into a car with an attractive woman with long dark hair."

Hatch made a mental note of this and listened intently as Willow continued.

"Then the lies came. The report went on to say that Kaitlin was a party girl and that she had run away from time to time. I told my husband to correct the report. I can't figure out why anybody would say that about her." Willow rubbed at her eyes again. No tears fell down her reddened cheeks. "The cops ate it up. I read the report. They made it sound like my daughter had run away. She has never run away in her life. Something is wrong. This makes little sense if any at all, and now it's been two days. Why won't they do something?"

Hatch could only offer pursed lips and a slight shake of her head in response.

Willow slid out a gray matte business card from a small hand purse on the bench beside her. "Here's the contact info for Gibbons. He gave me several of these and told me to give them to anybody who might know something." She looked down at the card and then back up at Hatch. "You're the first person I've given the card to."

"Thanks." Hatch pocketed the card.

"What are you going to do now?"

"I'm going to talk to Gibbons, see how best I can help."

"He seemed decent at his job when I talked to him. He was a Phoenix detective for years. But then again, I'm only going off what my husband told me. I'll let you be the judge of that."

"Do you have a number where I can reach you?" Hatch asked.

She took out a pen from her purse and jotted her number down on the back of the card. "This is my cell. I use it to keep in touch with my friends from the past." She held Hatch's gaze for an extra second.

Hatch read between the lines. Whatever life Willow Moss had before marrying her husband had been severed. Abuse came in different forms, each devastating in its own way. This was a *survivor* cell phone, a connection to her past she had just given Hatch.

"I won't use it unless I need to. I don't like making promises. But if I find anything, I'll let you know."

"I just realized I never got your name."

Hatch thought for a minute. Should she give Willow her actual name? The real Rachel Hatch had been burned alive and left for dead in Colorado. Does she exist to this woman who's now exposing the truth of her own life? Willow Moss has spent most of her adult life in a world of lies and deceit. Hatch did not want to add to another one to it.

"My name is Hatch, but..."

"But what?" Willow asked.

"It's better if nobody knows I exist."

"Well, you said you spoke to Williamson."

"I did."

"But you didn't give him your real name?"

"I did not, and I'd like to keep it that way." Hatch felt exposed by revealing her last name. She gave no first name or background story to fill in the gaps. A risky move, but sometimes honesty is the first step in building true rapport. She needed this woman to trust her.

Hatch stood. "I best get going."

"Me too. Kyle likes to track my whereabouts." She stood. "Oh, by the way, Teddy had that coming for a long time. Thank you for kicking his ass." The hardened look on her face softened. "Please help Gibbons find my daughter."

Hatch knew better than to promise, but she saw the desperation in the woman's eyes and leveled a serious gaze. "I'll do everything in my power to bring Kaitlin home."

TWELVE

THE FOG WEIGHED HEAVILY on her, as though she were waking from a dream. But she was lucid enough to understand her current situation was anything but a dream. This was beyond any nightmare she'd ever had. Whatever drug they'd given her lasted long enough to keep her in a semi-unconscious state for the drive. There was no account for the gap of time that had passed and no way to reconcile it. There was no watch on her wrist, no phone that she could check, and no clock on the wall. At least, no clock she could see in the darkness swallowing her.

She worked to piece together the fractured parts of what she surmised had been a day, maybe a day and a half of travel before stopping here. She guessed she'd been on the move for closer to two days by the light and dark filtering through the cracks of the cargo hold she was being transported in. Nothing seemed to make sense as she tried to make sense of a synchronistic timeline.

Her gut told her not to get into that car. Why did she? They didn't force her. They didn't put a gun to her head. Her entire life she believed that, if faced with those hard choices, she would always make the right one. Her mother and father had taught her well. The "stranger danger" warnings of her youth made her wary of the evil man with his van, luring in children with lollipops and candy, and did little to prepare her for a genuine threat. It didn't happen like she'd seen in the movies. They'd wined and dined her. They made her feel like it was her choice to make. And she had been the one who insisted. As she sat with only the cold damp air to blanket her, she wanted to kick herself for being so gullible, but her legs wouldn't comply.

Replaying the moments leading up to her captivity, it seemed like the script of a terrible B-movie. But she fell for it— hook, line, and sinker. Why would a talent agent stop her in a mall? Why would she even entertain the idea that that's how Hollywood stars were found in the Phoenix suburbs? How many girls had this woman approached before her? How many had been smart enough to walk away? It didn't matter now. Liz had wanted it to be true so badly, she could taste the lifestyle.

Her parents had always filled her head, telling her she was movie star beautiful. She wanted to believe them, but never really did. Her last boyfriend did little to reaffirm her self-confidence after sleeping with her best friend. Her parents doted on her and put in her mind that she had leading lady qualities. They made promises. Ever since she was young, her parents told her that when they got the money together, they would put her in acting classes. Talk of finding a talent agent to help her pursue those dreams had been discussed at length on several occasions.

Her life built up to that moment in the mall as she walked by a kiosk selling overpriced sunglasses in the center aisle. It was there that a gorgeous woman approached her. It startled Liz when the woman said, "Excuse me, I don't mean to bother you, but you're absolutely stunning. Has anyone ever told you that?"

Liz had been told that by a few people in her life, but Derek's cheating had scarred her and left her in doubt. Hearing this compliment from a beautiful, random stranger was more impactful. A validation at a deeper level, one she'd always sought.

That compliment stopped Liz dead in her tracks. The woman opened the portfolio she had tucked under her arm. Liz recalled how quickly the woman flipped through the pages of headshots and magazine cover shots. "These are just a couple of the people I work with. Maybe, you've seen them in TV commercials or as extras in movies? I don't know if you recognize any of the faces."

The faces seemed familiar, but none rang a bell. One thing was common among all the girls and boys shown—they were some of the most beautiful people she'd ever seen. Liz remembered being awestruck that the woman held her in the same light. Really? Her? Had to be a mistake. A fantastic, wonderful, life-changing mistake.

"Now some of them," the woman went on in a very professional, business-like manner, "have moved up and are actively working with the biggest producers in Hollywood. I can't say who, but Michael Bay comes to mind."

Liz's heartbeat tripled at hearing that. Could she be the next Megan Fox?

The woman continued, "You have the potential to be right in there with them. If you're up for the challenge."

Liz's mind nearly exploded.

She looked at the pictures and then back into the welcoming eyes of the beautiful woman holding the portfolio. There was no hint of sarcasm. Liz remembered looking around to see if she was on a practical joke TV show or if she was the subject of a prank by one of her friends. She could see her friend Mandy coming up with something like that. But there was nobody around. No cameras. It was just her, this woman, and the other shoppers moving about, paying them no mind. She'd borrowed her parents' car for the trip to the mall and was otherwise alone.

"Now listen, you're probably thinking this is a scam,"' the woman had said. "And I totally get that. I want you to know that this is on the up and up. If you're concerned at any point or you don't want to talk to me any further, please tell me and I'll leave you be. But if you're interested, I'd be more than happy to speak with your parents. I could set up a meeting with them, I've done that in the past. Anything to make you more comfortable, but I really see great potential. And this is what I do, I'm a talent scout."

Liz wished she could go back in time and choke the life out of the woman who'd landed her here. But that hadn't been her reaction at the time. In fact, at that point of the conversation, Liz's mind had already projected forward, envisioning all the money she could earn and how she could change the course of her life.

"Do you act?" The talent scout had asked.

"I can sing and dance a little. I did ballet for six years, but I play soccer now."

"Sports are great. That's probably why you've got such a toned, athletic build. And having a ballerina's background is always a plus. But singing ability is a big selling point. If you can really belt out a tune, there's a whole lot I can do to market you."

Liz was shocked this opportunity was being presented to her, but more so because this talent scout treated her like an adult. She'd be turning 18 in two months, but her parents still controlled most aspects of her life. They wanted Liz to go off and be the first in her family to attend college. They didn't have the money to send her to a big school and had pitched the idea of starting off with the community college near her house and later transferring to a larger university.

She knew her parents wanted nothing but the best for her but were extremely limited in their finances. Liz looked at this opportunity to pay for everything she wanted. She wanted to give her parents a better life than they could ever give themselves. She saw this as a chance to give back to her parents, who had given up everything for her.

Liz's parents' life had been on pause from the moment she'd been born one month premature to a teenage mom and a boy just about to enter adulthood. A typical mistake, but they took it on the chin like adults. Her father dropped out of high school and began an apprenticeship as a mason. Her mother finished school at night and waited tables at a dive bar a ten-minute walk from their apartment. Both put their dreams on hold. Over the years, her folks worked hard to give her a decent life. College was expensive and the last thing Liz wanted was to start off adulthood with a mountain of debt.

She'd spent most of her life watching her parents struggle and didn't want the same for herself. She wanted to help them out. And the way to do it presented itself while she was on her way to pick up a graduation dress at the mall.

A talent scout had picked her out of the crowd. Amazing. Out of all the other people milling about, this woman wanted her. She had even offered to call her parents. Instead of taking her up on it, Liz said, "I don't need to call my parents. I can decide for myself."

And in that moment, she had unwittingly sealed her fate and set in motion a series of events that led here. The talent scout offered to take her to meet her boss. The woman said this was the guy who could launch Liz's career, and he was in town.

Liz forgot all about getting her formal dress. She jumped at the opportunity and followed the woman to the parking lot. The last thing she remembered was getting into the passenger seat of an oversized SUV. Before the talent scout closed the door, she jammed a needle in the side of Liz's neck, leaving her frozen with shock. When she tried to move, tried to fight, her limbs didn't cooperate. Her body tingled with a warm sensation, followed by a cool rush. It was like she was underwater, and everything became muddled until it dissolved. The next coherent memory was of the heavy-handed bald man with a thick beard.

All her replaying of those events leading up to this moment did nothing to better explain where she was now.

After the truck stopped moving, they shoved her into a small room with a mattress on the floor. She fought back as best as she could, but they cuffed her hands behind her back. Whatever resistance she offered was thwarted. Thank goodness for the mattress on the floor breaking her fall. Without her hands to brace herself, she felt the impact of the concrete floor underneath.

The bearded man was inside with her and accompanied by another leaner man. "You girls keep your mouths shut while you're in here. Do you understand?"

It was then that Liz realized she wasn't alone in the dark cell.

"Don't say anything to each other. We're going to be moving out soon, and I don't want to hear anything when this door opens again. That clear?"

Liz's eyes further adjusted to the darkness. In it, she saw the other girl, set back against the far corner of the room, away from the mattress. Her knees were curled up into her chest and she rocked silently. Her red hair fell over her face, obscuring any of her features.

The bald thug with the thick beard wore a heavy gold chain that jingled as he walked over to her. Liz watched as the redhead cowered at the large man's approach. He then bent down and gently patted her head as though she were a dog who had obeyed his command.

Liz smelled it before she saw it. It was then that she realized how hungry she was. Her stomach's rumble was loud. The smell of burgers and fries filled the small space, invading Liz's nostrils. Then, she saw the Wendy's bag in the bearded thug's hand.

"Here you go. Don't eat too fast or you'll make yourself sick." His voice was tender, the softness of which was unsettling.

The redhead didn't reach for the food, nor did she say anything.

"I'm going to move your cuffs to the front so you can eat more easily," he said. "But to do that I have to uncuff one side and bring it around to the front. Don't do anything stupid while I do this. Do you understand?"

The girl's red hair bobbed up and down once.

There was a gentleness to the way he talked to her, an intimacy. The redhead said nothing as the man moved behind her and undid the cuffs. Liz looked on, thinking what she would give to get an arm free so she could try to fight her way out. She watched as the redhead offered no resistance while the bearded man locked her hands back in place in front.

"Don't worry. It'll get better soon." He offered this encouragement before bringing himself upright. Standing erect, he towered over the room.

The younger thug stood near the door and said nothing. The big man looked over at him and laughed. "See, I told you, she just needed to be broken in a bit. There's no fight left in her now."

The two chuckled quietly to themselves as they walked out. After shutting the door behind them, Liz heard the loud thud of a deadbolt and the sound of their feet thudding on concrete as they walked away.

"What the hell is going on?" she whispered.

The redhead said nothing. With the door shut, almost all the ambient light had been removed. In the darkness, Liz could hear the crunch of the paper bag the food had been delivered in. The foil wrap covering the burger crinkled as she opened it.

Over the next few minutes, Liz listened as the girl scarfed down every bit of food like a ravenous dog. Once the chewing stopped, the redhead spoke. "If you want to survive, just shut your mouth and do what they say. Do you understand me? They won't hurt you if you don't resist. I wouldn't fight them if I were you. You'll end up dead. Or worse."

Liz contemplated that statement for a moment. "What's worse than death?"

The redhead didn't offer an answer initially. It came in the sound of a long exhale that transformed into a whimper. "Just trust me on this. Some things are worse than death."

Liz shuddered as her mind raced for an answer on how to get out of this place.

THIRTEEN

AFTER WILLOW DROVE OFF, Hatch placed a call to the number on the card. Colton Gibbons answered, sounding as though she roused him after an all-night bender. Unlike Williamson, Gibbons seemed eager to help and agreed to meet Hatch. He suggested they meet at the Songbird, a coffee house in downtown Phoenix. Gibbons said he'd be there in twenty minutes. Hatch mapped it on her phone and would be there in less than seven minutes.

She caught a long red light which delayed her. She was still ten minutes ahead of the time Gibbons suggested. Hatch liked to arrive early for any occasion. She took a right onto 3rd Street from E. Garfield and pulled up alongside the curb near an empty lot about four spaces from the coffee shop.

She waited inside the car and looked around. A few high-rise apartments littered the view. An empty lot with a graffitied low concrete wall abutted the coffee shop's south side. Across the street was a small youth theater. An older model Jeep Wrangler parallel parked two spaces from Hatch. There was a small PT Cruiser between them. She guessed the man in the driver's seat to be Gibbons. He was early too, by five minutes.

Gibbons stepped out into the bright surroundings. Hatch took a moment to watch the man without alerting him to her presence. Watching the private detective's wobbly exit, she gauged her initial assessment of his drunken stupor was accurate.

He leaned against the front of the Jeep and dug around the pocket of his shirt. He pulled out a box of Marlboro Reds. She watched as he snapped off the filtered end between his fingers. Gibbons stuck the unfiltered cigarette into his mouth, lit it, and took a long drag. The gray wisps of smoke blended with the man's ashen complexion.

She waited for him to finish the cigarette before exiting the car. Hatch did this not only to avoid standing in the man's smoke, but to assure he hadn't brought unwanted company to their meeting. Satisfied, she approached Gibbons.

He flicked the cigarette into the middle of the street and pushed himself off his car, balancing uneasily. Hatch noticed he favored his left leg.

"Gibbons?" Hatch asked.

"The one and only, at your service." Gibbons performed a mock theatrical bow. He then opened the driver's side door. A moment later, he popped back out with a notepad and pen in his right hand. A cane was in his left. "Shall we?" He gestured toward the coffee shop.

Hatch nodded. She berated herself for misjudging the unsteadiness of the private detective's stance as a sign of intoxication. That lasted until she was close enough to smell him. Gibbons reeked of scotch.

They went inside and Gibbons bought Hatch a coffee. They took a bench outside under the shade of a tree in the small courtyard. Gibbons sat across from Hatch. He rested his cane against the adjacent seat and took a sip from his coffee. He did not try to hide his stare and Hatch made no attempt to mask the mangled, twisted roots of the scar tissue lining her right arm.

"Fire or shrapnel?"

"A little bit of both," Hatch offered.

"What was the tattoo that used to be there?"

She glanced at the fractured quote. "It's still there."

"What was it before you had it redone?"

"A quote from Alice in Wonderland."

"Really?"

"What's it to you?"

"IED?" he asked nonchalantly.

He was either socially inept or had experienced trauma firsthand. Hatch would have to peel back the layers to get the answer to that question. She nodded again, not wanting to offer details. But her visual presence was cause for conversation.

"You ex-military or somethin'?" he asked.

"Let's focus on Kaitlin Moss. That's why I'm here. And that's why the Moss family hired you. Who I am, what I am, has nothing to do with this case."

"Fair enough," he said. "I can see you like to get down to the brass tacks. Me too." He opened his notepad. "Let's hear what you've got."

She told him everything and shared the photo files from her phone. The date-time stamp on the image she'd taken from the gas station surveillance camera showed they were now three and a half hours from the last known sighting of Kaitlin Moss.

Hatch was left to gather as much information as possible from the man seated across from her. Besides the fact that she was legally dead, she didn't have a network at her disposal. She planned to call Savage, but any favor she asked could lead back to him or her family.

Fort Huachuca was the home of the 111th Military Intelligence Brigade where Hatch had spent countless hours learning the tradecraft of human intelligence, or HUMINT. Those connections had long since evaporated, leaving Hatch to rely on Williamson and Gibbons. Sadly, the ex-cop turned private detective who stunk of scotch and smokes with a hint of black coffee and looked like he slept in his rust-covered car was the better of the two options.

Hatch didn't want to judge Gibbons too harshly, though. Too many people had judged her based on appearances and come up on the wrong side. She decided to give Gibbons wiggle room to see what he was made of.

"What do you plan to do with this information?" she asked.

"After this, I'm going to run the info through my connections. I have good friends still with Phoenix PD that I can reach out to. Although it's against the rules, they'll run the plates for me. Then I'll go from there."

"Go from there?" Hatch said.

"Yeah." He took another sip of his coffee. With each pull of the drink, he seemed to come more alive. His booze induced cobwebs dissipated. "Listen lady, I know you see a frumpy crippled private detective. You're probably thinking burnout. Maybe I am. But I'm probably the best chance the Moss family has of finding this girl. I find those who can't be found and have succeeded in that for the past five years."

Hatch took a sip of her own coffee and raised the other hand up to stop him. "I'm not passing judgment. I'm just trying to make sure whoever's looking for this girl is going to do it right."

"Like I said, I'm the right guy for this whether you see it or not."

"Is the pay commensurate with the level of work? Or do you always smell like a distillery by midday?"

He almost got up. Hatch watched his hand curl into a fist. "What I get paid is none of your damn business."

"I'm sure you didn't present yourself to the Moss family like this. Yet here you are two days into the investigation of their missing daughter, and you appear to have spent several hours of it keeping your blood alcohol level up."

He threw his hands up. "You don't know shit." A couple at a nearby table looked up from their frothy lattes. Gibbons lowered his tone. "Until you walked into my life, I didn't have jack on this case. Everything I'd gathered up to this point was leaning in the direction that Kaitlin ran away."

"That doesn't jibe with what Willow told me about her daughter."

"I know. I talked with Willow. She doesn't believe her daughter ran away."

"And you?"

"I thought she was overreacting at first, but considering the information you've just provided me, I believe she's in real danger."

"Need any help?"

His eye cocked up. "You wanna help with the investigation?"

"If you don't mind."

"I do mind. I work alone. I got a secretary who handles the administrative stuff. Not looking to pick up any strays."

"I wasn't asking to be your secretary. I asked if you wanted my help. Without going into any details, I am qualified to find people in danger."

"Not interested. I don't have room for a wing man, or wing woman, whatever you'd call it."

"I don't think you'd find me to be a burden," Hatch said. "Why don't you call Willow and ask her if she wants me to help."

Gibbons huffed and angrily sipped at his coffee. "So that's it. You want a piece of the Moss fortune. You're just like every other nimrod who's called in her location."

"I don't want their money. And I don't want anything from you except to tag along." Resolution to this situation might be found without Hatch assisting beyond this point, but she needed to be a part of this. She wasn't sure if this need was just her longing to reconnect to a world she understood. Regardless, this missing girl mattered. And whether Hatch wanted to admit it openly or not, it gave her a renewed sense of purpose.

"I'm not paying you a thing. That money she paid me to find her daughter is my money."

"Again," Hatch raised a dismissive hand, "I said nothing about money."

"Well, you know they're rich as hell."

And then she saw it. Whatever Willow was paying him, he was holding out for a bigger payoff at the end. The reward money was the ultimate lure for the detective. It didn't mean he'd do a half-assed job. The opposite might be true, but Hatch was convinced of one thing: she wasn't leaving until Kaitlin Moss was located.

"You were a detective, right? Every detective I ever knew had a partner who lightened the load, whether it was as simple as one doing the interview while the other typed the warrant. And it's always good to have two sets of eyes on surveillance."

He chewed on the thought for a moment while taking a long, last drag on his cigarette and crushing it out and flicking it five feet away. "As long as you understand that, then I guess an extra hand couldn't hurt. Sorry, old habits. I've been running solo for the past few years. I guess I'm not used to working with people anymore." His fist relaxed. He left a sweat mark on the wooden tabletop next to his coffee cup.

"If it's any consolation, neither do I.".

"To be honest, you're the first breath of fresh air that's blown into this case since it came across my desk. I was starting to run my head into a wall." He paused long enough to gulp down the rest of his coffee. "Those cops interviewed a bunch of students. What they said about Kaitlin being a bit of a party girl who'd run off with some friends didn't make sense to me. But I could only go off what I had. Zilch. The information pointed the finger at a dark-haired woman in her mid-twenties, apparently the last person Kaitlin was seen with. She admitted to never seeing Kaitlin before. Seeing her in that SUV with those two men gives me a lot to be concerned about."

"And rightly so," Hatch said. "I just wished I had acted sooner and directly helped her when I had the chance."

"Don't beat yourself up over it. How were you to know?"

"Well, that's why I need to see this thing through."

"We'll see where things go, but if you piss me off, I'm kicking you out of my car. I don't care if we're in the middle of the desert. As long as you understand me on that, things will work out fine."

"You won't need to shove me out in the middle of the desert." Hatch offered a weak smile. "Let me help you find this girl so I can get on with my life and you can get back to yours."

"Why do you care so much? I mean, I get it. Missing girl and all. But why go through all this trouble?"

"Everybody should care about a missing kid. I don't enjoy seeing bad things happen to good people. And when I'm able to do something about it, I do."

"Kind of like your civic duty, huh?"

"More like a code I live by."

This seemed a sufficient answer because Gibbons pulled out his cell phone. He winced as he turned to adjust himself in his seat. Whatever malady required he use the cane still looked as though it caused him pain. "Hey Mike, it's Colton. Yeah, yeah. Hey, look, I got a plate." He paused while the man on the other end spoke. "Don't give me that. This is a real one. This one matters. I got a plate and you're going to run it. You owe me."

Hatch was happy to see that his charming personality was not only reserved for her, but even close friends. A few seconds later, Gibbons jotted some notes on his legal pad. Hatch watched his nicotine-stained fingers fidget with the pen in his hand. He was jonesing for another filterless cigarette right now. Hatch thought about spending the potential hours sitting in a car with the chain-smoker. It would be but a small sacrifice if it meant finding the young girl.

"Right here in Phoenix, huh? Okay, Mike, thanks." Gibbons clicked off the phone and finished up his notes. His handwriting could pass for a doctor's and Hatch had difficulty reading it.

"Is that a leasing company?" she asked.

"Yup. It returns to Tripoli Meat Distribution. It's a meat packing company here in Phoenix. Not too far from us. We could probably be there within fifteen minutes depending on traffic."

"Why are we still sitting here?"

"My sentiments exactly." He gave a half smile as he picked up his crutch and forced his body's girth to an upright position as they ambled out to the sidewalk where their cars were parked.

"I assume you want to ride with me?"

"It'd be a lot easier than following."

Gibbons opened the passenger side door of his Wrangler and scrounged around the floorboard. He popped back up with an empty yellow packaging from a bag of peanut M&Ms. He outstretched his hand. "Stick this under your driver's side windshield wiper and park your car across the street, in the lot beside that youth theater."

Hatch took the crinkled wrapper. 1429 was handwritten in black ink on the inside. "What's this?"

"Old trick, but still works. Put your badge number on the inside of a peanut M&M wrapper. Meter maids know it's a cop's car and won't ticket."

"Why peanut M&Ms?"

"The yellow packaging makes it easier to see. Especially at night." Then Gibbons' mouth widened into a smile. "That and I love them."

Hatch did as he suggested. Two minutes later, she was seated beside Gibbons in his rundown Wrangler, heading to a meat packing plant that held the first potential link to the missing Kaitlin.

FOURTEEN

HATCH AND GIBBONS sat under the minimal shade of the twisted branches of a tree a hundred feet from the main gate entrance of the Tripoli Meat Distribution packing company on S 17th Street of the Sky Harbor Industrial Business Complex. They were nestled in a sea of nondescript warehouses. The vantage point from their position gave a decent enough view of the comings and goings, but the high walls and surrounding buildings restricted their ability to see beyond.

There was no sign of the SUV from the Gas-N-Sip. Patience was more than a virtue. But every passing second still felt like Kaitlin was slipping further away. Each minute passed like hours. The silence between her and Gibbons only added to the strain of it.

Hatch hoped this partnership would be short-lived and would bring resolution to the missing girl.

There were several vehicles, mostly large shipment trucks, coming and going. No SUV and no sign of the men who Hatch last saw with Kaitlin. Most people moving about the grounds of the plant were men and women in blood-covered white overcoats or well-dressed foremen. This first potential lead was looking bleak.

That was the thing with surveillance; the most disciplined reaped the reward.

Gibbons used the time to forward the images of the suspects to his counterpart at Phoenix PD, even though he wasn't hopeful they would recognize the shady men. Hatch didn't have high hopes either.

Upon completion of his task, Gibbons stepped outside to take his third smoke break since arriving. At least he was courteous enough to step outside of the vehicle. Proper surveillance would have dictated he stay in the car, but the thought of inhaling the filter-less Marlboro Reds for hours on end would've driven Hatch to the brink of insanity. So even though she didn't agree with his actions, she was grateful, even if he carried the residual odor back inside each time.

He drew no attention as he lingered outside of his Wrangler. Standing by a junked car wasn't out of the norm for the environment they were in. He looked like the other workers in the area who similarly ventured out to take their smoke breaks. No one noticed. No one cared.

Hatch and Gibbons watched and waited. Gibbons plopped into the driver's seat and looked over at Hatch. "What happened to your arm, *Daphne?*" He put the emphasis on her name. She wondered if Willow had already betrayed her trust. Maybe it was Gibbons prying. Always the cop, trying to figure out who she really was, suspecting she had given a false name.

She didn't bite. "Long time ago. Doesn't matter now."

"I meant no offense." Gibbons threw his hands up in surrender. "Just making small talk. When you sit here for a while, not much else to do."

She'd been on many a surveillance op. She'd known the passage of time always moved faster with pleasant conversation.

"I get it. Just not much for talking about it." What she really meant was that he hadn't earned the right to hear that story. She doubted he would earn the right in the limited time she planned on spending with him. "If you want to talk, tell me the story of why you left the department. Your card says twenty years of law enforcement experience. Did you get your full retirement?" She eyed the cane, guessing the answer.

"Nah, I made it seventeen years. Figured I'd just round up. With my private investigative stuff added in, it gets close to that number, right?"

Hatch shrugged. "I'm not judging. What happened?"

He sighed. His turn in the hot seat, but unlike Hatch, he didn't pass. He braced himself against the steering wheel, gripping it tight for a second before releasing. The air conditioning dried the beads of sweat as they popped up along his receding hair line. "It's a long story."

Hatch stared out the window toward the meat packing plant. "Looks like we've got time."

"I was working overtime when it happened. There was a turf war between two local crews. They'd been battling it out on the streets for several weeks and the bodies were piling up. Lots of pressure to get results.

"We were on the scene of our second shooting of the night and the Freemont Boys were responsible. I was in Homicide back then, but I'd worked a few cases against them in the past when I was in Narcotics. I reached out to an old snitch and he tipped me off on where the shooter was holed up. My partner and I went to check it out."

"Just the two of you? Wouldn't that be a SWAT call?" Hatch regretted the questions as soon as she'd asked.

"You seem to know a lot about police work."

"Movies," Hatch offered, unsure if he bought it.

"Guess so." Gibbons chuckled and fell into a brief coughing spell, no doubt courtesy of his unfiltered Marlboro red habit. "I was pushing the envelope by going after this guy without an army of backup. But I weighed the greater good. I couldn't let that punk shoot another person and I feared by the time we launched a coordinated plan, he'd be in the wind."

Hatch understood this drive better than the ex-cop would ever know.

"We got to this abandoned apartment where the killer was supposedly hiding. My partner held his position out front. I went through the alley around back. Son of a biscuit was coming out when I rounded the corner. Must've seen my partner." Gibbons paused. His right index finger rubbed against his middle. "He got the first shot off before I could get my gun out. Hit me here." Gibbons tapped his left knee. "Knocked me on my ass. I didn't even realize I'd fired my gun. I was shocked later when I learned I had popped off seven rounds.

"He fired two more times before dying. The last shot shattered my hip. Thank God it missed the femoral or I wouldn't be sitting here now.

"Getting shot is a weird thing. I tasted the gun smoke before I felt the pain of the rounds that entered my body. I tasted the heat of it before I heard it. He hit me three times before I could go for my weapon. All the hits were below my waistline. I've replayed that night a thousand times in my head since."

"How long did you stay on after?"

"I was thinking about riding it out on a desk but that wasn't where I was at. Kind of went against how I had spent the first seventeen years. I was always a street guy, even when I was in the Bureau. I liked to be out there. And I don't know, I guess when I realized I wouldn't be capable of performing the job the same way, I decided to take the medical retirement."

Hatch wanted to speak. His story echoed hers in many ways. Although under different circumstances, she had taken the med-out option as well once her old team had turned their backs on her. She wondered if Gibbons' teammates and partners did the same to him.

"I just couldn't do it my way anymore, so I left," he said.

"You're out here now," she said.

"Not the same. Most of what I do in my current position doesn't require much in the way of extensive field work. I usually just have to snap a couple pictures of a cheating spouse. Not really danger zone kind of stuff."

"I could see where that would get old after working the kind of cases you were accustomed to handling."

"Don't get me wrong. The benefits are good. It's just the boredom that's killing me." He flicked an empty pack resting on the center console. "And these things. If I had to guess, boredom will get me first."

"Just don't go dying before we get Kaitlin back."

Gibbons smiled. "Well, aren't you a compassionate one?"

Hatch let out a laugh. It had been a while, and it felt good.

"This is going to sound weird, but I'd rather take a case like this any day. Aside from the work of it, I get to keep in touch with the guys from my old unit. Helps me connect to the source."

Connect to the source. She'd felt that same disconnect when first departing the military. Part of it would always be there. Going back to Hawk's Landing had enabled Hatch to reconnect to an old source, to her life before. Her home had enabled her to remember the version of Rachel Hatch from before the taint of her father's death and the things she'd endured after. It called her to a simpler time. But her need to find out what had happened to her father had permanently erased the possibility of pursuing that life. She was adrift again, disconnected from the military and from Hawk's Landing and the people left behind.

Hatch looked at her watch. It was 2:30 PM, six hours since she had seen the girl in the gas station. A lot of ground could be covered in six hours. They could be anywhere. Every time she thought of the unknown timeline working against them, she felt a sense of desperation. Had Hatch not been who she was, she would have labeled it as anxiety. Her tension felt more like a snake coiling, ready to strike. She needed a target to sink her fangs in.

Gibbons saw her eye the time. "I know what you're thinking, but let's hold out hope. Getting across the border with a young girl and without papers is going to be hard for them. Only thing we can do is focus on what we can control, and that's what we're doing here now."

"I know it's just—"

Gibbons flashed wide-eyed for a moment as if her statement gave him an epiphany, but before he spoke, Hatch saw why.

The driver from the gas station stood out among the crowd of white meat packing jackets. He didn't get into the same vehicle as she'd seen earlier. This time he got into a lime green Maserati. He revved the engine twice and pulled out of the lot quickly, almost recklessly as he sped away from the meat packing company.

Gibbons winked, "Looks like your lead paid off."

"We still have to catch up to him first."

Gibbons put the Wrangler in drive and gave chase.

FIFTEEN

"EASY," Hatch said. "We don't want to scare him off."

"I know what I'm doing. I was born and raised around here, and I know these streets like the back of my hand."

Hatch defaulted to his expertise.

Gibbons took a right while the Maserati continued straight. "I'm going to stay parallel to him. Watch this, he'll never see it coming."

The Jeep's six-cylinder engine roared as he took a left, doglegging onto the parallel road. The Wrangler was faster than she'd expected.

"She looks like hell but drives like heaven." Gibbons chuckled as he propelled the Jeep forward.

The traffic was lighter on this road and there were fewer stop lights. Hatch was impressed. She got a sense for the type of cop he must've been. One of the ways you could gauge this was by how well they knew the streets. The rusted Wrangler was now nearly side by side with the Maserati. Only a block separated Hatch from one of the men who'd been directly involved in the abduction of Kaitlin Moss.

The vehicle disappeared and reappeared from behind the buildings they passed. Through it all Gibbons kept up, matching the sports car's speed. He then whipped the wheel to the left hard enough Hatch thought they might topple over. Soon they were barreling down a one-way alley toward the Maserati.

"Got a cut back over here. It gets tight up ahead. Should keep his speed in check." He slipped into the Maserati's lane, leaving one car between them. "Don't think he saw us."

"I don't either," Hatch said. She was watching the eyes of the driver ahead, looking for the telltale twist of the head to check his mirrors, but there was none of it. He was oblivious to their presence behind him. She wondered why he was so careless, and then she realized with a pang of dread that whatever involvement he had in Kaitlin's abduction had been completed. Hatch didn't allow her mind to go down to the dark place where experience was trying to lead her.

"She's not with him," Hatch said.

Gibbons kept his eye on the vehicle in front of him, maintaining his tight tail of the Maserati. "What do you mean? How do you know?"

"Look how he's driving. He doesn't care. He's not even monitoring his speed. He's been fluctuating between five and ten miles over. What professional driver, if that's what he is, would do that with a package onboard?"

"Sounds like those movies you watched sure taught you a lot about police work," Gibbons scoffed.

"What do you want to do?"

"He's our only chance of finding out anything." His pale face focused on the car ahead. "And we need to speak with him. I've got an idea."

"I'm all ears."

"Two blocks up, these two lanes merge. There's always fender benders. The traffic unit affectionately named it Crunch Ave."

Hatch gave a slow nod, getting what he was saying. "When you ram him, let me grab him."

"Whoa, whoa, whoa, hon. Didn't say anything about ramming him. What do you think this is, the Army? We're not overseas, soldier."

He must have figured the military angle because of her arm and the way she reacted to the comment about the IED. *He has a good read on people*. There might be more to this man than she'd originally given him credit for.

"I'm just going to have a little fender bender. Tap him, make it look accidental. Then we'll help him out of his car and into ours." He winked, putting Hatch at ease.

Not only had she misjudged him, but she also liked him. His ability to come up with this plan on the fly proved that he'd been a good cop, willing to take risks to do the right thing. Same as her. They were cut from the same cloth.

As they approached the merge, Gibbons made his move. He acted as if he was planning on turning left and pulled into the turn lane alongside the Maserati. He hung back enough to remain in the blind spot of the sports car.

At the merge, Gibbons turned back into the lane, banging the rusty Wrangler's bumper into the left rear quarter panel of the small lime green Maserati. The impact was harder than Hatch had expected, and it sent the sports car skittering sideways pinning it against a bolted mailbox.

The driver exited. His face was red, but he barely looked toward the Jeep. Instead, he rushed to the backside of his vehicle and knelt beside it, as if tending to an injured child. He looked more hurt and worried than angry, and then he looked up at Gibbons, who was getting out of the Wrangler and approaching.

For a man on a cane, Gibbons moved quick. The kidnapper looked confused. And was about to speak but stopped as his eyes moved past Gibbons and locked with Hatch's.

She was already sprinting forward out of the car as the driver began running back to his dented Maserati. She came alongside Gibbons, when the Maserati peeled out and off into traffic, nearly clipping a small Taurus entering from an intersecting street.

"What the hell happened?" Gibbons said.

"He recognized me. He saw my face."

"He saw you from a gas station six hours ago and could recognize you after getting sideswiped?"

"Thinking what I'm thinking," she said as they jumped back into the Wrangler.

"These guys are pros." He dropped it in drive and gunned it forward.

Gibbons slipped in and out of traffic with the Maserati leading the charge. The driver was skillful. So was Gibbons. He was matching him move for move, outsmarting the driver of the more powerful sports car. Gibbons navigated the streets of downtown Phoenix with the familiarity of a spider navigating its spun silk. She hoped the fly they sought would remain in their web. Each move Gibbons made brought them closer.

The driver of the Maserati was reckless, but that love and tenderness that he had shown for his dented fender caused him to approach the intersections with a bit too much caution. As he came up to a red light with thru traffic already crossing, he slowed. Gibbons saw the opportunity and slammed his car into the same dent area. This time not sideswiping. His Jeep struck the Maserati at a perpendicular. As the Maserati tried to push forward, it spun. The spin stalled the vehicle out and it went into reverse while in drive.

Gibbons rammed the front, forcing the back end of the Maserati into a light pole. This time the smaller, faster car was trapped. In one deft move, Gibbons had outmaneuvered and pinned a professional criminal driver.

Hatch was already on the move. She could see the driver, though stunned, was reaching down towards the center console as Hatch came up to the window. She saw the butt of a gun. He never had the chance to grab it.

Hatch struck down hard with her right hand, the impact rippled along the scar tissue and damaged nerve endings of her arm. But it felt good. It felt even better when she dragged the man out of the car. The best feeling came when her forearm crashed down on the side of his neck, rendering him unconscious.

She grabbed him under his armpit, stabilizing his neck against her stomach as she pulled him out. Hatch and Gibbons each took up a side. Acting as human crutches, they moved him to the rear of the Jeep, away from the stopped traffic's view. They then tossed him in the back seat.

Hatch followed behind, securing the unconscious man in a wrist lock while Gibbons got into the driver's seat. He tossed her a set of handcuffs from the glove box and peeled away.

SIXTEEN

GIBBONS DROVE to a warehouse outside of Phoenix. It had taken them forty-five minutes to get there. They had exited the main road and driven down an unpaved dirt road that led on for the last ten minutes of the trip, bringing them to a warehouse in the middle of nowhere. Like an oasis rising from the desert, an old, dilapidated building appeared. Not unlike the one where she'd confronted the outlaw motorcycle gang in Luna Vista, New Mexico. Her experiences circled back like life playing on a deja vu loop.

Hatch covered the captive with a throw blanket that she found on the floorboard. It was oil-stained and smelled of mold. But it sufficed. He'd begun stirring a few minutes out from their crash. He moaned and whimpered at first but offered no fight. Hatch slid the blanket off, exposing the bound man to fresh air for the first time since he came to. After that, he offered no resistance and remained in a curled position with his head against the opposite side door.

As the vehicle came to a stop, their captive bucked. His eyes pleaded with Gibbons.

"I wouldn't get any ideas if I were you," Hatch said. "Your hands are secured in handcuffs, but I didn't double lock them. That means you start rolling around in here and those things will bite down tight. I've seen them cut into bone. Understand?"

He nodded. His clothes were soaked through with sweat. Hatch hadn't removed the blanket out of kindness. If an interrogation were to take place, she wanted to build rapport. Subtle gestures paid big dividends in an interrogation.

"She's gonna take that gag off," Gibbons said. "You and I need to have an understanding. The windows are up and we're in the middle of nowhere. Any scream for help you make is not only a complete waste of your energy but will cause further harm to you. You don't speak unless I ask you a question. And you damn well make sure you think about anything that comes out of your mouth before you open it."

The captive man stared at Gibbons, his eyes pleading. Gibbons' warning coupled with the seriousness in his pale face quelled the last bit of resistance. Their prisoner remained scrunched into a half-fetal position. Hatch twisted her body and reached down to the belt used to secure the musty cloth to his mouth. She released the belt and returned it to her waist. The dirty rag that was packed tightly into his mouth fell onto the floorboard and for the next minute, the man in the back seat said nothing. He breathed deep and slow. Once his body had calmed, he looked at both of his captors.

"Sit up nice and slow," Gibbons ordered.

The dark-haired prisoner did as instructed. "What is going on?"

Gibbons struck out with the quickness of a viper. His movement even catching Hatch off-guard as he slapped the man on the side of the head. The impact was loud in the tight confines and the right side of the tanned prisoner's face reddened. The blow caused his eyes to water. "What did I tell you about talking?"

The prisoner broke eye contact and lowered his head.

"You know what you did to land you in the position you're in right now." Hatch was soft-spoken but controlled. "You've done a bad thing and we're the people you're going to talk about it. I don't want to talk here in this Jeep. This isn't the right place for that. What you need to do in the limited time you have left before we walk into that warehouse is think hard about how well you want to cooperate with us because it will determine the rest of your day and possibly your life."

"You a cop? Cops don't talk like this. Who are you?" He stuttered the words. Hatch turned toward Gibbons. She wasn't sure if his outburst would result in another slap. Gibbons' hand flinched but remained out of play.

Hatch had slipped into her old role. She'd used the time prior to the impending interrogation to develop a base connection to their prisoner. She wanted him to see her as his lifeline. If he felt she held his life in her hands, Hatch would have a more effective platform for extracting truths. She wanted his trust to outweigh his resistance. This rapport building used by interrogators worldwide to establish a connection between captor and captee was a variant of the Stockholm Syndrome.

During periods of captivity, prisoners develop a psychological allegiance to those holding them. This theory came to light after a 1973 bank robbery in Stockholm, Sweden, where the four hostages refused to assist in the prosecution of the robbers. Points and counterpoints had been logged over the years as to the causative factors for their allegiance. And even though the Diagnostic and Statistical Manual of Mental Disorders, the bible of mental health disorders, has never formally accepted it, the theory is widely accepted.

Hatch had dealt with numerous hostage recovery operations in her time with the military and had witnessed it firsthand. It was pervasive, not only with hostages, but with victims of domestic abuse and sexual assault. In the role of captor now, she wanted to use those subtle gestures to manipulate Kaitlin's kidnapper into submission.

They hadn't had time to discuss this next phase, and Hatch was curious about who would lead the interrogation. She'd already slipped into her old role, forgetting herself and exposing a glimpse of her experience. In the limited time she'd had with Gibbons, Hatch had seen his police skill set shining through his shambled exterior.

Hatch automatically had gone into autopilot, using her subtle gestures of kindness during the car ride to plant the seed of trust. It's what she'd done on many high value target extractions overseas. Experience paved the way for her ability to extract information from people who had no intention of providing anything. And she did it better than most.

"Don't worry. This is the right place." Gibbons' ashen face screwed up into a half-cocked smile. The words had an equal and opposite effect on the imprisoned man.

Hatch shifted their prisoner to the side and retrieved his wallet. She pulled out his license. "Alejandro Dominguez, is it?"

Dominguez rubbed his face against his shoulder, wiping away the pool of sweat perpetually forming before nodding.

Hatch scanned the area. The only other thing in sight besides the warehouse was a broken-down repair truck with four flat tires and a sidewall decal so faded its words were unreadable. The exterior of the warehouse was covered with old graffiti tags. Hatch was confident nobody had used this space any time recently. A desert landscape branched out in all directions as far as she could see. The two-story warehouse was set into a low point, obscuring its view even more so. This was an ideal spot for an interrogation.

Gibbons and Hatch exited the vehicle. He left the engine running, closed the door and crutched himself over to Hatch. He leaned against his cane and pulled a cigarette as the two stood in front of the noisy Wrangler's front end.

He spoke softly between puffs of his Marlboro. "How do you want to handle this? Sounds like you got a little rapport going with him. But it's best I take a crack at him. I know his type and I can play the bad cop when I need to."

"This is your case. I'm just here to help if you need me." Hatch eyed the warehouse. "I'm guessing you didn't just stumble across this place."

"Raided it years back when it used to be a meth lab. After we shut down the operation, they passed it from owner to owner until nobody wanted it anymore. Maricopa County bought it for an additional gun range and training facility for their sheriff's office, but it never got off the ground. Budgeting or something. After a while it became a hangout for the Narcotics guys. A place where we could come, like a clubhouse, and decompress."

"How long were you in the Narcotics game?"

"Long enough to know it's a game with no winner. And long enough to know that it's a shell game between the money and the drugs who control it. I saw a lot of strange things in the four years I worked in that unit."

He looked at the warehouse as if recalling a memory. "It took me a while to see it, but our unit wasn't really looking at taking the drug dealer off the street. The priority in which we selected our targets was based on how much money they would bring our department. The cash seizures were all they cared about. Eighty percent of the money seized came back to the PD and the additional 20 would go to the state. We timed our hits to achieve this. Our goal was to hit the dealer when they were product light and cash heavy."

"Policing for profit," Hatch mumbled. She knew of it, but her Army police experience had been different.

"Call it what you want, but our unit was the only one earning our salaries out of the seizures we made. Hell, the department benefitted. One coke ring seizure afforded us a new fleet of patrol cars. I know everybody's got their opinion on it, but it's just the way it was. I got burned out and took a detour in Homicide. I guess solving murders was more cut and dried." Gibbons flicked his cigarette off into the distance. "Enough about me. It's time we had a little heart to heart with our guest."

"Agreed."

"Why don't you get him out and bring him in the building. I'll get things set up. Figured since you already got the groundwork rapport established, you can use it to establish primacy before I begin my interrogation."

Hatch noticed the word choice. By using the term primacy, Gibbons was testing her. It was a technique used in the early stages of interview to establish a primal dominance over the subject. Typically, this psychological dominance came in the form of highlighting an investigator's enhanced abilities to detect lies or solve a case. In its most basic sense, it was a game of mental intimidation. Hatch debated on feigning her lack of knowledge but decided against it. Gibbons was catching wind of her level of experience, and she decided not to offer any push back.

"Will do." Hatch hoped she just passed Gibbons' litmus test of understanding interview and interrogation. He walked away saying nothing further.

Hatch went back around to the driver's side, cut the ignition, and pocketed the keys. The Jeep's temperature rose at least ten degrees within seconds of the air conditioning turning off. Had time been on their side, Hatch would've let the man sit and bake for a while before taking him out. That was not the case. Every second mattered.

She went to the rear door of the Wrangler and opened it. "Up for a little hike?" Hatch asked lightly, making it seem like there was an option. And there was: walk or be dragged. Hatch felt the measures to intimidate countered her goal of softening their prisoner and making him open to suggestion. She hoped the softer approach would help make Dominguez open to communicating.

He slid himself out of the Jeep and rested his cuffed hands against it for a moment. "You don't have to do this," he whispered to Hatch as she grabbed him by the left elbow.

Hatch didn't answer. She guided him forward toward the door Gibbons had entered moments before. As they got closer, she felt him tremble. He was terrified. This could be taken advantage of. "I hope you've considered what we talked about. About answering honestly."

He nodded. About halfway between the Jeep and the warehouse, he slowed his gait.

"Don't even think about it. There's nowhere you can run out here that I can't catch you."

"I wasn't gonna run," he said between ragged breaths. She saw his chest was rising and falling more rapidly now. He was becoming consumed by the fear of what potential horrors that warehouse held.

"I'm not here to hurt you."

"I'm not so sure about that," he said. "People don't get abducted and thrown in the back of a car and brought to an empty warehouse in the heart of nowhere for conversation."

"We'll talk inside."

"I don't want to die."

"We'll talk inside," Hatch said again, ushering him forward with the tight grip on his elbow. His statements sent a chill down her spine. Was he laying out the girl's fate?

"You're just going to kill me." He was nearly inconsolable and had forced himself to a complete stop at this point.

Hatch thought about shoving him forward but thought better of it. Getting him moving again under his own control was the better option. "Listen to me carefully. The man inside wants to have a conversation with you. And so do I. It's an important conversation. One in which your answers dictate the outcome. Know what's at stake when we walk through the doors of that warehouse."

Dominguez swallowed the dusty air around them and his eyes watered.

"If you lie to him, he will know. He is single handedly the best interrogator that I have ever seen. He's gotten some of this state's most notorious criminals to confess. And you don't fall into that category." Hatch delivered the primacy statements on Gibbons' behalf.

"Why are you telling me this?"

"Because I need you to understand that when this conversation begins, there's no point in lying to us. If we suspect you're lying, this may be the last door you ever walk through."

" You said you weren't gonna hurt me."

"I said we don't want to hurt you. Don't leave that choice on the table for us." Hatch guided him forward. "That choice will have direct and awful consequences. For you, mostly. The best decision you can make is to put one foot in front of the other and walk yourself into that room. Sit quietly and listen to what we both have to say. And when my partner asks you a question, answer it honestly. If you do those things, your day is going to get a lot brighter. If you do anything else, if you try to protect the people we want to talk to you about, you'll find yourself in a world of misery you've never experienced before in your life."

Hatch moved in close to the man's face. She made sure his eyes met hers. She made sure what he saw in her eyes was nothing but the cold, hard truth. Dominguez began moving on his own again. Hatch loosened her grip slightly as they proceeded into the warehouse.

Colton Gibbons sat behind a metal table. There were two chairs, one beside him and one opposite. Hatch guided Dominguez to the folding chair across from Gibbons and gave the private detective a slight nod, letting him know that she had done as he had asked.

"Well, Mr. Dominguez," Gibbons said. His voice crackled, a combination of the dry air and continual cigarette smoking that left him with a raspy hiss punctuating each sentence. "Treat this like the first day of the rest of your life."

SEVENTEEN

THE MIDDAY SUN penetrated the cracks of the poorly maintained warehouse. Through broken windows, beams cast areas of the building's interior in their white light. Particles of dust floated, air currents lifting them in swirls. The makeshift interview table was kept in a hazy darkness away from the room's natural illumination. There was no electricity, and even in the dry Arizona climate, the air carried dampness. The mustiness held a hint of urine.

It was warm, but better than outside. The concrete slab flooring helped maintain a natural coolness. The table looked like crackheads had used it for a card game. Scribbled markings covered every inch. Gibbons now used the tabletop to rest both of his forearms as he leaned in towards the man seated across from him.

It was Dominguez who spoke first. "Is there any way that you could loosen these cuffs? I swear to God, they're slicing through my wrists."

Gibbons looked at Hatch and she walked over to inspect. She slipped her pinky finger in the gap between the wrist bone and the stainless steel of the cuff. She did so for both wrists and then said to Gibbons, "He's fine."

"They're not built for your comfort," Gibbons said.

The finger's gap was enough to allow for normal blood flow along the wrist and therefore no long-term harm.

Many police departments had been sued for excessive force because of improper handcuffing techniques. Hatch had learned how to secure the most violent offenders without making their wrists an issue. No reason to destroy a great case with improper technique.

"What do you guys want to know?" Dominguez asked. The agitation in his voice overriding the fear she had heard earlier.

"We know what you did. We know who you are. We just need to know where the girl is."

"What girl?" Dominguez broke eye contact. "I don't know about a girl."

Gibbons shifted in his chair and was about to explode across the table. He was quick with the backhand in the Jeep, but in the more formalized interview setting, he showed restraint.

Dominguez refused to meet Gibbons' stare and turned his head in Hatch's direction.

"Stop looking for her," Gibbons said. "She can't help you. I can help you. But only if you talk about the girl."

"What do you want me to say?"

The tension in his hand whitened his knuckles as Gibbons' cigarette-stained fingers curled into a fist. Hatch thought for a second that he was going to strike the man. She knew that beating confessions out of people didn't always work; the mind can resist physical torture more easily than the psychological attacks. Time wasn't on their side. Hatch had used physical means to expedite an end in the past but knew there were more effective ways of extracting truth.

"Where's Kaitlin Moss, the blonde girl you and your buddy abducted?"

"There's nothing I can tell you that will change things. It's done. She's gone."

"I want you to explain to me where you took her after your stop at the Gas-N-Sip. I want you to be very clear in details that will help us find her." Gibbons banged his fist on the table. "And God help you if you tell me one more time that you don't know what I'm talking about."

"I don't... I don't know..."

"You don't know?" Gibbons seethed. "Two seconds ago, you were asking me what girl I was talking about. Now you're telling me you don't know where she is. So, what is it? Didn't my partner explain anything to you before you came in here? If you don't tell me the truth, you're good as dead. I'll leave you here. I'll leave you here to rot. When's the last time anybody's been through this warehouse? Go ahead, take a guess."

Dominguez shrunk, as if being called to the board by a teacher to answer a problem he hadn't prepared for. He scanned the floor and the walls around him as if the answer would magically appear. He gave a simple shrug of his shoulders. "I can only tell you what I know."

"Better be good. This place might as well not exist." Gibbons gave a wicked smile. "Do you know how long you'd last in here handcuffed to that chair without food and water? Have you ever seen somebody die like that?".

"You said as long as I—" Dominguez started.

Gibbons cut in. "I said you had to talk. Right now, you're hemmin' and hawin' like you've got a choice in the matter. The only chance you have of walking out of here again and seeing the light of day is if you open your stupid mouth and start explaining to me where Kaitlin is. There's no time to play patty cakes with you when there's a little girl out there who needs our help." Gibbons then lowered his voice. "If you don't have the answers I'm looking for, we'll have to leave you and find somebody else who does. Oh, and I'll be sure to leave the door open when I go. Animals that come through at night might need a midnight snack."

Hatch watched as the tremble she'd felt when holding his elbow extended to his entire body. "I'm just the driver, man. That's all I do. I drive."

"From the looks of it, you might be up for a career change. She spotted you at the Gas-N-Sip. Not a smart move stopping with the girl. And secondly, my piece of crap Wrangler caught your ass. Maybe whoever you work for needs a new driver."

Dominguez sniffled loudly. A combination of snot and sweat combined to give him a translucent mustache.

"He's not interested in helping us. Ready to go?" He looked past the man to Hatch, who remained standing guard behind their prisoner.

"I'm ready if you are." Hatch played along.

Gibbons grabbed his cane and shifted in his seat.

"Wait." Dominguez sat up. "I'll tell you everything I know."

"What do you mean? You said yourself you don't know anything. You're just a driver. We must've been wrong to assume otherwise. I don't want to waste your time, Mr. Dominguez."

"Seriously, I'll talk. I'll tell you everything I know. Just don't leave me here."

Gibbons released the cane in his hand. It clanged noisily against the metal back seat of the adjacent folding chair.

Hatch had played along with Gibbons' act, knowing it was a ruse. He gave her a subtle nod of approval before focusing his attention back on the handcuffed man seated before him.

"Well, assume that I know enough to know when you're lying. Assume that you're about the shittiest criminal I've ever met. You can't hide a thing from me. This conversation isn't like any interview you've ever been through, so get that into your thick skull. We're off the grid here, meaning nobody knows where you are." Gibbons traced his index finger along the scribbled tags on the tabletop in front of him. "And if I get annoyed with you, if you're lying, then I will put a bullet in your leg. Do you like how that looks on me? You want to walk with a cane for the rest of your miserable, pathetic life?"

Dominguez shook his head wildly. He made a strange sound as he choked back tears. Gibbons had tapped into a palpable fear. The gravity of the situation seemed to have finally sunk into their prisoner. Dominguez was primed.

"They, the people I work with, are going to kill me. If I tell you any of this, you might as well put that bullet in my head 'cause I'm already dead."

"We've already crossed that bridge. You're in a warehouse on the outskirts of Maricopa County in the middle of nowhere surrounded by an unforgiving landscape. They can't make you any more dead than I can. At least with me, you have a chance of coming out of this thing alive. Maybe you'll live long enough to die another day."

The brick of Dominguez's defensive wall crumbled. Gibbons had knocked down their prisoner's barrier. Hatch looked on, impressed with the former detective's ability to manipulate the situation to his advantage.

"I was recruited after a stint in county a while back. Caught the attention of a couple people with how I handled my time. They needed a driver and I fit the bill. That's all I do. I move the product."

"The product?"

"The product, that's what they call it. They sell girls."

"What happens to them?"

"After they're sold? I'm not sure. These girls fetch big money, but I don't know much more after I deliver them." Dominguez dipped his head. "I do know the girls I transport are never seen again."

Hatch's stomach turned. It had been almost six hours. Where was Kaitlin Moss? Her mind raced, but she didn't interfere with Gibbons. He'd gotten Dominguez to open up this far.

"Where is the blonde girl that you had in your car earlier today? Did you know there are pictures of you and your friend with that girl at the gas station? How stupid are you that you stopped with a 'package,' as you call them, in your backseat?" Gibbons admonished the driver.

Dominguez's body language told the story. His shoulders rolled forward and his head dipped low like a flagpole at half-mast.

"The world is going to become a lot smaller place for the people you work for," Gibbons said.

"Shit," Dominguez muttered. Tears fell, splattering on the graffiti covered table in front of him.

"Stop your blubbering," Gibbons said. "It's not gonna change a thing. I need the information that's going to save that girl's life and yours. So, spill the beans. Where did you take her?"

"Nogales."

"Mexico?"

"No. Nogales on the Arizona side. There's a motel just outside of it called the Sunnyside. It's where I drop them. What they do with them from that point isn't in my wheelhouse."

"You said them?" Gibbons asked. "How often do you do this?"

Dominguez shrugged. His cuffs clanged against the backrest of his chair.

"How often?" Gibbons leaned in, the intensity in his voice matching the expression on his pale face.

"I don't know. A lot."

"What's a lot to you?"

"Sometimes twice a week, sometimes a few times a month. It depends on the demand."

"Demand?" Gibbons parroted.

"It's just how it works. I get a message telling me where to go. My partner and I scoop up the girl."

"How do they pick the girls?"

"Again, that all depends, too. I don't get into the how of things. I just receive information once they've selected a package for pickup."

"A target location? What are you guys, special forces?" Gibbons wise-cracked.

"No. But it's a big business, and it's run like one."

"A business? You abducted a seventeen-year-old girl so they could sell her into slavery. Don't try justifying it."

Dominguez was quiet for the next minute. "Look, I'm a two-time convicted felon. I've got nothing else going for me, but I can drive a damn car. Forgive me for not taking the moral high ground, but for the first time in my life I finally had more than two pennies to rub together. I know it's wrong. But I'm just trying to survive."

"You said the name of this motel, the one you drop the girls at, is called the Sunnyside?" Gibbons eyes were a blend of controlled fury and strange compassion.

"Yeah. The company owns it. They run it like a regular motel, even keep a couple rooms available for random travelers. It's done to keep outward appearances on the up and up. Most of the rooms are used to house the product until they're shipped off to the next location. It's basically a holding area."

Hatch worried if she heard Dominguez call these girls packages one more time, she was going to choke the life out of him. She fought to control her rage, knowing the detrimental effect it would have on extracting the right information and undo all Gibbons had accomplished so far.

"Why the meat packing company? Is that where you work?"

He let out a loud, slow sigh. "No. It's where I tell my parole officer I work. The company got my name on their payroll. The meat plant is legit, but it's owned by the same people who run the girls."

For the first time since this interview began, Gibbons was speechless.

"How much time after you drop a girl at that motel before they've gone for good?"

"Like I said, it's really not my job—"

"Just tell me what you know. I don't even care if it's hearsay. Give me something."

"One day. Two at max. They get them situated, drug them up so they don't fight, and then start to condition them."

"Condition them?"

"It's the final phase before they ship them off to the buyer." Dominguez sat up and looked drained. "I dropped her off at the motel about two hours after she saw me at the gas station."

"Who runs this thing? Who's the boss?" Gibbons asked, squinting his eyes at Dominguez.

"No way. Doesn't matter what you do to me. Speaking his name is a death sentence. He'll sic the Ghost on me."

Gibbons eyes flashed. "What'd you say?"

Dominguez cowered. "Nothing."

"I have half a mind to put a bullet in your head right now." Gibbons pressed, but this time Dominguez didn't back down.

"Guess so." Gibbons reached for his cane and motioned to Hatch. "Let's go."

"But I told you everything I know. I told you the name of the hotel where I dropped the girl. What else do you want me to do?"

"I want you to die." Gibbons stood up.

"Wait. I told you everything!"

"Good luck in your next life," Gibbons said as he walked away toward the door.

Hatch said nothing to the handcuffed kidnapper and fell in behind Gibbons. He closed the door and they walked toward the rusty Wrangler.

"Give me a second." Gibbons held a hand up as he opened his door. "I need to call a friend."

Hatch understood and stepped back, offering privacy.

Thirty seconds later, the conversation was over, and Gibbons waved her in. "Sorry about that. This friend is particular about our conversations."

"I take it this was not your friend from before?" Hatch wanted to take it back. She knew better than to push a cop, past or present, to reveal their contacts. Those connections fueled investigations.

"Different agency. He's just particular about how we do things." Gibbons shrugged. "I forwarded him the picture of Dominguez and told him of the connection to the meat packing plant. They'll be by to pick him up for a more formal interview and interrogation later, but it'll be good for our friend to sit for a little while and think about his actions until they get here."

"Fine by me," Hatch said. "Bastard has been helping sell girls. I couldn't care less if the coyotes come to take him home."

"Well, we got a few hours between us and Nogales. If you're up for the ride."

"There is no place I'd rather be." The stink of his Wrangler never smelled so good as they sped off, leaving a wake of dust spiraling behind.

The plumes erased the warehouse from view as they drove south toward Kaitlin Moss' last known location.

EIGHTEEN

ABOUT THIRTY MINUTES outside of Nogales, traffic slowed, and Gibbons pulled out his phone. "Mrs. Moss? It's Gibbons."

Hatch could hear the woman's voice through the phone, but the rumble of the Jeep muffled her ability to make out the words being said.

"We're on our way now. I'll keep you posted." He finished the conversation with, "We'll do our best." Ending the call, he looked over at Hatch. "She said to say thank you."

"Nothing to thank me for. We haven't found her yet."

"The past two days have been a nightmare for her. This is the first ray of sunshine in an otherwise dreadful forty-eight hours. She's just grateful, is all."

"I know." The fact was, Hatch didn't. The closest she'd been to knowing what motherhood felt like came from her recent reconnection with her niece and nephew. Maybe if things had been different, she would've had a family of her own at some point. There was still time. She'd wished it could have been with Savage. But that would not be possible. He was there, and she was in the middle of nowhere with a man she barely knew and trouble she could have only imagined when she pulled into the gas station earlier that day.

Hatch's life until now consisted of fractured moments in time. She had accrued a lengthy list of life's unexpected deviations since the days of her youth.

"That's a good thing you did there," Hatch said.

"What's that?" he asked and looked as though he were awaiting the punchline.

"Keeping Willow informed." Seeing Gibbons handle the Dominguez situation, Hatch deemed him worthy of more of her trust and she felt comfortable revealing herself to him. "I've worked with a lot of investigators in my time, and while each was different, few took the time to keep the victim's family in the loop during an active investigation. That extra step is, in my opinion, the single most important trait. One that separates the great ones from the good."

"Did you just tell me in a roundabout way that I'm a brilliant investigator?"

Hatch laughed. "Don't let it go to your head. And I never said anything about brilliant."

Colton shrugged it off and followed with his signature cough. "I never really thought of that before. I used to do it back on the force. Old habits and all. I just always tried to put myself in the place of the suffering families. I figure even the smallest crumb of hope can carry them forward. Now, I'd never lie. But if hope is there, even fleetingly, they deserve to have it."

"Well, I'm sure Willow appreciated it."

"Least I could do, since now I'm being paid by the case. Figure I've got to prove up and show them I'm earning the money they're giving me."

He punctuated his last comment with a laugh, but Hatch saw his humor as an attempt to mask the fact that he cared. He was the kind of cop who cared, retired or not. The drinking and chain smoking couldn't mask the real man lying beneath the shroud of stereotypical escapism. Gibbons wore his burden like a superhero's cape. But after everything she'd witnessed of the man up to this point, Colton Gibbons had proved himself to her as not only a great cop, but also a decent human being.

Hatch admired those two unexpected traits she saw in the man seated in the driver's seat.

The Jeep bumped, jostling her mind from the wayward path it had drifted. She looked upon the barren landscape as they closed in on Nogales. She wasn't sure what was in store for them once they got to the motel. In the last couple hours with Gibbons, Hatch learned the retired cop could handle a racecar driver and run an interview. What Hatch didn't know was whether he could handle himself on the tactical end.

Trusting somebody's intuition and investigative skill didn't always transfer when things hit the proverbial fan. Hatch wasn't convinced he would be physically capable of keeping up. She hated herself for even thinking it. A big chunk of her doubt came from his damaged leg. Hatch rubbed her scarred arm. Many had passed judgment because of her injury, and their woeful mistake had surprised those people. Regardless of the reason, not knowing Gibbons' capabilities with the tactics side bothered her more than any potential misjudgment.

This wouldn't be a first for Hatch. She'd worked with others in the past, like Jabari during her time in Africa. She had even had her doubts about Savage when they'd first met, but he'd quickly proven himself. But this was a different circumstance. In the past, there had been time to build trust. The rapid unfolding of this current situation didn't allow for that build up. Hatch hoped Gibbons could hold his own.

"Maybe we should surveil first," Hatch said.

"First? As in before we go kicking the doors? You must see somebody else when looking at me. I'm good at a few things. Even decent with a gun, but I'm no Chuck Norris. You will not see me kicking ass and taking names. Those days have long since passed me." He tapped at his belly and chuckled softly, breaking into a short-lived coughing fit.

"Then what's the plan?" Hatch asked.

"Simple. We'll get eyes on the place and verify what Dominguez told us. If we gauge he's not lying and our girl's still there, we'll get local law enforcement to come in and do the rescue. No need for us to do it."

"What if they fail? What if we wait too long? Are you willing to hedge your bets that by the time you call it in, she'll still be there? It could take them too long to put together a tactical team and get to the motel."

"These things take time, if you want to do it right."

"I just don't want to sit around and wait. I want to get her out of whatever hell she's in, and I want to do it now."

"Where did you come from?" Gibbons cocked an eyebrow.

Hatch dismissed the comment. "Are you up for it? Because you're a hell of a lot more capable than you're letting on." Hatch eyed the cane and looked down at her right arm.

"Thanks, I guess."

"Or at least you could be." She looked back at the near empty bottle of Macallan rolling around on the rear floorboard.

"It's still a few miles to Nogales. I'd hate to see you walk it." He flashed his anger. "Why don't you hold your personal judgment before jumping to any conclusions?"

Hatch didn't defend her position. She allowed the venting without offering a counterargument. Whatever invisible ails plagued Gibbons' mind, they were just beneath the surface.

A wheeze accented the sound of his exhale. "Sorry," he said after a brief passage of uncomfortable silence.

"I get it, I crossed the line. I know I've only known you a few hours, but I can see good in you. Just look at the depth you're going to in order to help the Moss family. You've put yourself in harm's way and you took a huge risk bringing me on to help. You're selling yourself short."

Gibbons was silent again, but the flash of anger she'd seen moments before dissipated. "How about we get down there and see what's what? Once we get eyes on the place, we can verify if Dominguez was telling us the truth."

"And if he wasn't?"

"I'd say we'd have ourselves a major problem." A sour smile pressed his pale cheeks upward. "If that's the case. I'm going to pay him another visit. But if he's telling the truth, if the girl's there, then we'll do everything in our power at that point to weigh the risk versus reward about going in ourselves."

"Fair enough."

"What'd you do before? The way you talk makes me curious about the things you've seen and done."

Hatch felt that moment of vulnerability. She felt like she was back in the diner for the first time with Savage. The first time she opened up to him about her scar, about what caused it, even if she left bits and pieces of that tragic moment to herself. Here, on this ride to Nogales, the opportunity was presenting itself again. It was a chance for Hatch to connect on a human level. Gibbons had openly shared the traumatic experience that left his left leg lame. Now it was her turn. Like two medieval knights at a crossing, Gibbons had raised his visor to expose himself as a friend.

Hatch prepared to speak. As she did, the radio disc jockey interrupted the classic rock playing in the background with a breaking news update. Gibbons turned up the volume.

"Listeners in the Nogales area: A wildfire has broken out. Local fire and police are on scene. From a source at the Nogales PD, a man high on crystal methamphetamine lit himself on fire and drove his car into a liquor store in the One Thousand Block of North Grand. Apparently neither the crash nor the fire put an end to this lunatic's drug-induced rampage. An officer gave chase to the naked flaming man as he ran into the wood line behind the store. The subject died shortly after his apprehension. The store is now fully engulfed in flames. The car was loaded with several cans of gasoline. No other deaths resulted, but several employees and customers were injured. Anybody in the area is being advised by Nogales Police and Fire to evacuate. Those who decide to shelter in place do so at their own risk."

Hatch looked over at Gibbons.

"That's going to be a bit of a problem," Gibbons said.

"How so?"

"The Sunnyside Motel is only a couple blocks away. Means local law enforcement are going to be stretched thin assisting the fire department in closing off roads and evacuating homes."

"Looks like it's going to be up to you and me," Hatch said.

"It's worked out for us so far. Hopefully, our luck will hold."

NINETEEN

THE FLOW of traffic leaving the city increased exponentially. Gibbons impressed her with his knowledge of the city as he got off the interstate and navigated the back roads and bypassed the detours caused by the wildfire. The radio interruption about the man on fire interrupted her response to Gibbons' probe into her backstory. Although she embraced the idea of letting him in, she was grateful at the missed opportunity.

The Wrangler was now parked on a side street abutting a Chevron gas station. A few trees lined the curb, separating the street from the gas station's lot. Shade was no longer a necessity as darkness fell, but it helped to obscure their position from view.

Each second weighed on her as Hatch stared at the motel across the street.

This strip of Nogales had seen better days. A vacant building peppered with broken windows decorated the landscape to the right of the Sunnyside. The motel looked to be in marginally better condition than its surroundings. If what Dominguez had said was true, then even the rooms left vacant for weary travelers would remain vacant. *Smart move.* Making the place uninviting was a level of subterfuge that would aid in masking their operation.

There were two mid-sized sedans and a dark Chevy Suburban parked in the lot. The lot itself was a disaster with grass breaking through the cracked asphalt, standing knee high in spots. Hatch counted nine rooms in a u-shape. The glowing red letters underneath the motel's sign showed vacancy.

There had been no movement since their arrival. Had it not been for the three cars in the lot, Hatch might've thought the motel was abandoned. There had been no additional vehicles moving in or out of the lot and no pedestrian traffic. For a brief time, a scantily clad weathered prostitute lingered near the vacant lot on the right. But it wasn't long before an older man in an Oldsmobile picked her up and drove off.

Three of the rooms had lights on, but with the curtains drawn it was impossible to see inside. Gibbons had retrieved a pair of binoculars from the glove box. Even with the enhanced advantage, he could not see anything. The only person they could see was an attendant who passed into view from time to time at the main office.

Hatch knew the importance of surveillance, and the need for patience. She had proven herself in both her ability and stamina regarding patience. But this situation and her desperate need to protect an innocent girl had clouded her reasoning. Hatch wanted, *needed*, to be Kaitlin Moss' guardian angel. Maybe it had to do with leaving Daphne behind. But whatever the reason, her patience for waiting was slipping away.

"I'm going to go peek around," Hatch said.

"You're going to what?" Gibbons looked flabbergasted. "You're going to get yourself killed. Or they'll run off and that girl's gonna disappear forever."

"If she's even still there."

"Listen to yourself," Gibbons said. "Do you know how crazy you sound?"

Hatch wasn't used to being scolded when it came to tactics and was taken aback.

"This is still my show to run. And I'm telling you, you're not getting out of this Jeep until I say so. You will sit here and wait, just like me. Because it's the right thing to do. I know that you know that too."

She wanted to fire off a retort to put the retired detective in his place, run across the street, and kick in a door or two. But he was right. Gibbons was operating at a professional level. He allowed no emotional connection to the victim. She flicked her eyes to the visor mirror hanging down from the windshield as if it would give her an answer. On the outside, Hatch was the same person. But the ripple effect of everything that happened in Hawk's Landing had left her unbalanced. She felt its impact resonate in her now, at a time when she could least afford it. Hatch had to be perfect in judgment and action, just as she'd been before.

"You're right, but we need a plan of action should an opportunity present itself," Hatch said.

"Don't worry. I'm one step ahead."

FOUR MORE HOURS passed since darkness swallowed the daylight. The fire continued to rage on, casting the night sky an eerie pastel orange. It looked like the scene from a post-apocalyptic movie.

The fire seemed the only change since their arrival. The motel clerk had stepped outside to smoke on occasion. The lights remained on in the three occupied rooms. The flickering light from a television could be seen out of the middle room. Other than that, they were no further along in determining where or if Kaitlin was in one of them. The only solace came from the fact that nobody had left. If she was in there, Hatch was going to get her out.

Gibbons continued to take smoke breaks, but at least he did so from behind the cover of the tree trunk alongside the Jeep. It was a tactical no-no on any operation, and especially true when conducting surveillance, not to allow personal routine to interfere. But this wasn't a traditional tactical operation, and Gibbons, as great a cop as he was, was not a tactician.

Hatch had mentioned this to him about the cigarette smoking, and his response offering was, "Fine by me, I'll smoke in the car." To which Hatch then met him halfway and agreed that he should exit the vehicle.

As it neared midnight, there was no sign of change. It had been eighteen hours since she'd seen Kaitlin.

The smoke from his unfinished Marlboro Red trailed Gibbons as he pulled the door and hustled back into the car. "Movement. Middle room. Somebody's coming out."

Hatch was already watching. The curtain had moved back an inch. A shadowed figure filled the void. Backlit by the room, his features were washed out. "I got eyes on him."

"Let's wait and see what he does," Gibbons said.

A large barrel-chested man stepped out. He had a shaved head and a thick black beard that caught the glow of the sky. Adorned in a maroon velour tracksuit, with two white stripes down the outside of the sleeves, he wore gold rimmed sunglasses in the dark. The big guy looked as though he'd been imported from a mobster movie. As if adding the final piece to his character's role, he stood in front of room number two and lit a cigar.

"See, smoking helps," Gibbons said under his breath as they watched. "At least it got him out of the motel room."

"What do you make of him?"

"I mean, I don't know, looks like your classic Hollywood bad guy."

"Exactly." Hatch almost laughed.

"Maybe we should pay him a visit. I mean, operating strictly on hunch and all," Gibbons offered.

"I thought you weren't interested in getting hands on?"

He put his palms up, gesturing his defense. "No, you misunderstood. I said those days were behind me. If I'm reading you right, you can assist with that aspect. I can assist in other ways. Remember when we first met at the coffee shop?"

Hatch nodded, not sure where he was going.

"Did you smell the booze on my breath?"

"I did," Hatch answered without a hint of judgment in her voice.

"While it's true I enjoy my drink, I also use it as a stage prop."

Hatch was intrigued. She'd masqueraded herself into a variety of unique characters during her time, playing the role of prostitute in many sting operations. Gibbons had used a similar technique on her. Hatch was shocked she hadn't picked up on it. Was she slipping? "You mean you faked it for our meeting?"

"Smoke and mirrors. I play the burnout private eye rather good, huh?"

"Yes, but why?"

"It's an extra layer I use. Keeps people away. Apparently, it didn't work on you."

"I'm a hard person to shake," Hatch said.

"That's clear as day." Gibbons winked playfully. "I wasn't drunk this morning. Or hungover. I just swished a little whiskey around in my mouth before arriving." He pulled the collar up to his nose and gave an exaggerated sniff. "Even spilt a little extra on me for good measure."

"And the..." Hatch eyed the cane beside him.

"Nah, the limp's all real. But the rest of me, well, it's just a bit of an act I like to use. Keeps people out of my life and gives me the underdog advantage."

Hatch understood. As a female in the male-dominated world she chose, Hatch had used her underdog status to an advantage most of her adult life. "You said you had a plan. Let's hear it."

He reached back and grabbed the Macallan bottle. Repeating the process from earlier, Gibbons took a swig from the bottle. He then spat it onto his clothes, soaking his shirt and jeans. He took another swig. This time swallowing. "For the nerves," he said.

"I'll get that door open without having to kick. And when I do, that's when you come in." He reached over and opened the glove box again, this time pulling out a brown paper bag. He removed the Glock inside. Turning the butt toward Hatch, he handed it to her.

"From the way you talk, I'm guessing you know how to use a gun. But if you don't all you need to—"

"I know how to use it." Hatch seated the tang of the weapon in her left hand and did a quick press check. Satisfied a round was in the chamber, she tucked it behind the small of her back.

"You're a lefty?"

"I wasn't always."

He eyed her damaged arm and his slight nod indicated he registered her meaning. Gibbons picked up the binoculars and looked at the bearded man as he continued to puff away on his cigar. "This might not be the room."

The big man opened the door and reached his arm into the room. It reappeared a moment later with a stemless goblet of red wine. When the door was ajar, Hatch managed a glance inside. A blonde-haired girl was seated on the edge of the bed. The door closed and she slipped out of sight.

"Did you see her?" Hatch asked.

"I caught a glimpse, but it's hard to tell. She wasn't looking up."

"No such thing as coincidence in my world."

"Mine either." Gibbons set the binoculars down. "Looks like we've got work to do if you're ready."

"I'm as ready as I've ever been."

TWENTY

GIBBONS DROVE the Wrangler from the side street across the four-lane roadway to the entrance of the Sunnyside Motel. The clerk looked up from his desk as the Jeep pulled to a stop in front of the office. Hatch remained seated as Gibbons opened his door and stumbled onto the asphalt.

She had to admit, he was good. Hatch found his performance Oscar worthy. She watched Gibbons stagger in front of the Jeep as he progressed to the office door. Hatch did her part and slumped down in the seat, leaning her head against the cool glass of the passenger side window. They were just a couple of drunks looking for a place to crash.

The ruse had to be flawless if what Dominguez had told them during the interrogation was true. He'd said the motel was owned and operated by the company trafficking the girls. Gibbons needed to pass the clerk's litmus test.

Out of the corner of her eye, she kept tabs on Gibbons. He had worked his way into the main office and was now talking to the motel attendant. The act continued with Gibbons dropping his wallet while trying to make the cash payment for the room. A couple of minutes later, an unsteady Gibbons exited. He rounded the Jeep, dangling a room key in his hands like a dog treat. He winked at Hatch and slipped into the driver's seat.

"Room number eight. They offer a turndown service." He joked.

Hatch didn't laugh. The focus required for the task ahead was now settling in. She ran through the plan in her head. It was simple. The best laid plans always were. Simplicity minimized the risk of confusion that complicated operational plans often created. Less of an opportunity for Murphy's Law to creep in. Gibbons would put his acting talents to use again, this time to get the door open to room number two. After realizing he'd duped her during their first encounter, Hatch had little to no doubt he'd be able to pull it off. After the door opened, Hatch would do her part. She would be the tactical component of their plan.

Gibbons reached underneath the driver's seat and after a few seconds of fishing his hand around, he came up with a stainless-steel flask. He uncapped it and took a swig. He offered a sip to Hatch. She held a hand up and refused the gesture. "For luck?" He took back his offering.

"I don't bank on luck." Hatch looked toward the motel room where she'd seen the blonde-haired girl.

They waited to cross the motel lot until the large, tracksuit wearing gorilla retreated inside after consuming his cigar. Gibbons pulled up in front of room number three, parking next to the black Suburban positioned directly in front of room two.

The strong pungent odor of the cigar still lingered in the air outside as Gibbons exited. He leaned on the Jeep and grabbed his cane. "This is the point of no return," he whispered.

"I reached that the second they took her." Hatch slipped the Glock from the small of her back.

Gibbons stepped out with his cane and made his sloppy approach. Had it not been under such circumstances, his act would've been comical. He dropped his cane on the curb, and with it, the key to the room. He put on a good show for anyone watching.

He ambled up near the door to room two. Propping his cane on the left side of his waistline, he grabbed his pack of cigarettes and took one out. He broke off the filter of the Marlboro Red and placed the smoke between his lips. He took several drags while balancing himself precariously against the cane before he moved again.

Gibbons continued the drunken parody of himself. Watching it on full display, Hatch realized that his ability to pull it off so naturally implied that its origin came from an authentic piece of the former lawman's life. Experience was the best teacher. Gibbons' display demonstrated he was chock full.

With the cigarette still dangling from his mouth, Gibbons staggered against the door. He shouldered the door, making a loud thud. He then spun on his cane toward where he had dropped the room key. Hatch slumped down in the passenger seat with the gun resting on her thigh. Her right hand was on the handle with the door ajar.

Gibbons retrieved the key and wobbled in front of the door to room two. He was muttering to himself. He inserted his key into the room's lock and dropped it again. When he bent down to pick it up for the second time, he banged his head against the door and staggered back. Hatch exited the passenger side with the bootlegged gun at her side.

The door bolt released and in the small slit of the open door appeared the bearded man. Gibbons stepped forward with the key outstretched in his hand as he zig-zagged back to the door. Hatch staggered close behind.

The door to the room opened a little further, maxing out the slack of the chain lock still attached. "Wrong door, asshole," the bearded man said.

"It's my room," Gibbons mumbled. "Now get the hell out. I paid for it and you...you stole it."

Even under the incredible stress of the moment, Hatch had to fight the urge to laugh as her partner laid it on thick. Gibbons kept his head down when he made his next move and fell forward, slipping the cane into the opening.

"Get the hell out of here, you drunk son of a bitch!" The big man unlatched the chain and opened the door wide enough to push his arm out toward Gibbons. "Wait...What are y—"

Thanks to Gibbons' ruse, the door was now open. Hatch rushed forward, sidestepping Gibbons as she closed the gap. The bearded gorilla was dumbfounded by Gibbons and still in mid-sentence when she struck him on the side of the head with the butt of her Glock.

The impact dazed the thug and he stepped back, releasing his grip on the door, causing it to swing wide. Hatch was already in the room when he looked surprised to see her. She brought her boot down on the man's pelvis when a blur of movement from near the bed on the far side of the room caught her eye.

A fit, well-groomed young man had the blonde-haired girl in a choke hold from behind. Her matted hair covered her face. And in the split second she had to take in the scene, Hatch couldn't tell if she was even alive.

The gorilla fell back on an end table. His massive frame smashed the light atop it. Hatch kicked down hard. This time the bottom of her boot kicked hard on his face, crushing the gold-rimmed glasses and temporarily taking the big man out of commission.

Hatch shifted to address the hostage. The guy holding her now had a gun pressed against the side of her head while he inched back and disappeared into the bathroom. Hatch didn't have a clear shot.

Gibbons was in the room now and made his way over to the gorilla who still looked unconscious from where Hatch stood. Hatch moved to the bathroom door.

Hatch stood at the door for the fraction of a second it took for her to square herself to it before kicking it open. The clean-cut kidnapper's head filled the foreground of her front sight post. She fired twice, feeling the old familiar kick of the gun's recoil ripple through her body.

She blinked and realized the kidnapper was still there. The two rounds she'd fired had not impacted. *Impossible*. Her mind replayed it. She could see the gunshot wounds in her head and the blood splatter over porcelain tile. Yet here he was, unharmed and still holding the girl. The blonde-haired girl's body remained limp, but her head was now raised up and she was staring wide-eyed at Hatch. The gunshots must've roused her from whatever drug they gave her.

Hatch's eyes drifted down to the gun in her hand as she was struck on the right side of her head by a baseball bat. The blow buckled Hatch to her knees. Dazed, she raised her arm up but could not do so in time before she was struck again. At least this time she saw it coming. It wasn't a bat.

It was a cane.

And the last thing she saw before slipping into unconsciousness was the ghost white face of Colton Gibbons as he brought the walking stick down on her.

TWENTY-ONE

HATCH'S WRISTS were secured behind her back in handcuffs. The teeth of the cuffs were ratcheted tight enough to pinch her skin. Gibbons didn't take the extra second to ensure a fingertip's gap like she had for Dominguez.

"You brought this on yourself. You really did," Gibbons said. "You wouldn't be in this mess if you'd left well enough alone. But you had to go all Nancy Drew. If you had just passed along the information like a good little girl, then you'd be on your way back to wherever the hell it is you came from."

She was in the same motel room as she'd been when he knocked her unconscious. Somebody had moved her to a bed. Hatch was grateful she was still clothed. The blonde was passed out next to her. Hatch wasn't sure what hurt worse, the damage from the cane's blow or her mental beating she was giving herself for completely misreading Gibbons.

"Why didn't you just kill me when you had a chance?"

"Too messy. Too much potential for exposure," Gibbons said. "Plus, we need to figure out what you know."

"I know what you know." Hatch involuntarily reached at her throbbing skull. The handcuffs served a quick reminder that option was not available. "Nothing more."

"We're going to have to make sure you didn't leak this to anyone else. Like maybe your Sheriff friend in Hawk's Landing?"

Hatch's stomach dropped.

"I can see by that look in your eyes I touched a nerve. I ran your license plate. It seems a one Dalton Savage is the registered owner of that vehicle. Might be worth my while to pay a visit after this is all done. You understand how thorough I am."

Hatch fought the urge to strike out at Gibbons. She battled to mask the panic she felt. "He's just an old friend. I'm the only problem you've got."

"Even after the beating I gave you, you're still all piss and vinegar? Maybe I should give you a couple more whacks for good measure?" Gibbons sat on the bed across from Hatch and stood up quickly.

His cane was still resting against the broken nightstand. It took a second for her mind to catch up to the image of the man standing before her. His body was perfectly erect. There was no more gimpy lean, as if during her cane-induced sleep Gibbons had been miraculously healed. *Praise Jesus.* It was no miracle, though. He didn't need the cane. He had never needed the cane.

"That's right. I'm as able-bodied as they come." Gibbons showcased his left leg like a game show hostess revealing a new car.

Hatch refused to acknowledge Gibbons' taunts and looked to the girl on the bed. "It's not Kaitlin," she murmured.

"Nope." Gibbons shook his head from side to side in an exaggerated manner. "You can't let it go, can you?"

"I'm guessing there was a time when you used to care. You can't fake some of that stuff. It's in you. I know it."

"Whatever you're doing won't work. You're not going to appeal to my sensibilities and steer me away from the dark side. This isn't Hollywood. This is real life, sweetheart. So, save your psychobabble for somebody else."

"I'm not trying to play you. I know there's good in you. Maybe it's residual bleed over from another time in your life, but it's there."

"I've made my peace with who I am. You should probably do the same."

Hatch heard the not-so-veiled threat of things to come but didn't bite. She leveled an icy glare at the man she'd come to trust. A trust he'd built using a well-planned ruse. Hatch was working hard to counter her predicament with a plan of her own.

"And you've really pissed off some powerful people. You went nosing around in the wrong backyard and took what would have been a simple situation and made it a thousand times worse. So, they asked me to bring you in."

"Bring me in where? To who?"

"My employer would like to turn your annoyance into profit."

"What?" Hatch's mind reeled.

"You're going to be joining our next shipment of merchandise. I know you're damaged and an older model than most of our customers prefer, but my boss will find a way to profit from you. You're a feisty one and I think that'll help fetch a good price. Not a high one, but a good one. Good enough, at least. It won't be long until we take that fight out of you." Gibbons gestured to the unconscious blonde girl laying on the bed next to her. "See what I mean?"

Hatch shifted herself closer to the sleeping girl, who looked to be sixteen or seventeen years old. An innate need to protect her from this vile scum filled her. Even in handcuffs, Hatch vowed that none of these men would ever touch that girl again.

This girl could pass as Kaitlin Moss' sister. Her eyes opened halfway. Behind the drug-induced hollowness, Hatch saw the fear. Whatever they'd done to her since taking her captive would have an everlasting traumatic impact on the young girl's life. If Hatch could keep her alive. For now, Hatch was in her own hell and had to help herself before she could render aide to anybody else.

On the nightstand that served as a backstop for the kick she'd delivered to the bearded gorilla rested the Glock Gibbons had provided her.

She eyed it, remembering the two well-placed shots she'd fired into the center of the clean-cut kidnapper's skull. Bullets that never found their mark.

"That was the best part." Gibbons followed her gaze to the weapon. "You should've seen the look on your face when I handed you that gun. It was like you were ready to take on an army. Too bad I filled it with blanks."

Hatch choked back the rage rising inside her. She was mad at the deception, madder because she'd fallen for it. Hatch was furious at herself for not taking the magazine out. Had she done so, she would have seen the crimped green tip of the rounds and known they were blanks. When she did the press check, all it did was expose the rear of the casing, proving that there was a round in the chamber. She had seen it was in battery and ready for operation. The weight hadn't been off. A gun fully loaded with blanks as opposed to 180 grain ammunition has an imperceptible difference. Why hadn't she checked? The word soured in her mind as she called it forward. Trust. She had trusted Colton Gibbons. If Hatch's life experience had taught her nothing else, it was to trust and verify. She hadn't and because of that she was cuffed next to a girl she tried to save.

"I had to make it look good." Gibbons threw his hands up in mock apology. "I sensed from our conversations you came from a law enforcement or military background. Maybe both. I didn't want to leave anything to chance. These guys had no idea. Freddy didn't know until he opened the door that it was me." Gibbons looked over at the bearded two-ton gorilla standing guard by the door. His face now carried evidence of Hatch's fury. His nose broken and the side of his head swollen. Freddy seethed as he met Hatch's eyes. "I was hoping he would've realized and grabbed you. But you surprised all of us with your speed and skill."

"The cops have the same information I gave you. They're going to be coming."

Gibbons gave his signature raspy laugh. The laugh Hatch had grown to like was like nails on a chalkboard to her now. "You really think Williamson is going to track anybody down?"

"He's in on it too?" Hatch asked, not expecting an answer.

"No. He's just an incompetent moron. Easily led down the wrong path. Not unlike you."

Hatch bit her tongue at the stinging blow to her ego.

"We found out the information together."

"Correction. You found it out with me. Not going to lie, guiding you toward this end was no small feat. Probably my best ruse to date. One for the books."

"Well, what about Willow? She knows about me. She knows I'm here with you now."

"She'll get the tragic news soon. She'll hear how you bravely tried to save her daughter and ended up dead." Gibbons faked his limp again. "See? I'm just a cripple. I tried to help but couldn't. I mean, I'm not going to say it won't be a hard cleanup, but these kinds of things happen. And this is what I do best."

"Where is she? Where is Kaitlin?"

Gibbons let out an exasperated sigh. "Handcuffed on a bed surrounded by three armed men and you're still trying to play the role of savior? That's kind of cute, but your hero days are over. I don't know much about your past, but I will in time. I'm guessing your actual name isn't Daphne Nighthawk. Not that it matters. Because when I'm done with you, anybody who has any potential knowledge of this organization will need to be silenced."

Hatch thought of her family in Hawk's Landing and of Savage. She left home to protect them and still had placed them in harm's way once again.

"You've failed. I see the wheels turning in your mind. Get it through your thick head, it's over."

Hatch heard the words. They resonated with her differently. She was somebody not accustomed to failure. Her former team leader, Chris Bennett, had said those words to her after completing The Gauntlet for a second time. Those words continued to sting. Hearing them now from this man cut her like a knife. Even in the face of her current circumstance, Hatch was certain of one thing: Before her time on this earth ended, she would ensure Colton Gibbons was dead.

"Who else knows you're here?"

Hatch said nothing. She would give him nothing.

"I need to assure my employer the coast is clear."

"I guess that's a risk you're going to have to take." She thought about Savage. She was angry at herself for not reaching out to him about this situation she'd found herself in. What about Nighthawk? He was out there like her now, a ghost among the living. His past life erased and an unknown future ahead. Why hadn't she thought to reach out to him? Debts owed and honored; these were things both those men understood. They were things that Hatch understood. She had added Colton Gibbons to that short list, but now realized her folly. No backup was coming. Nobody knew, and there was no rescue party searching for her. It would be left to her and her alone to get out of this alive.

Hatch manipulated her hands, bound behind her back. In her time in the military, she had received a variety of survival trainings. One such course about street survival had been taught by an old crusty sergeant who told a story of a patrolman who was taken hostage during a routine car stop. During the altercation, the cop was handcuffed with his own cuffs. The instructor explained a simple preparation that would've given the compromised officer an advantage. He advised always taping a handcuff key at the small of the back. The likelihood of being handcuffed was slim to none, but if keeping a small handcuff key accessible could mean the difference, then why not do it. Ever since, Hatch had kept a cuff key taped on the inside of her belt. She ran her index finger along the leather of her belt until she felt it.

She couldn't access it right now with Gibbons watching. She was confident they'd done a thorough search and was glad they hadn't found it. And for that, Hatch had hope.

"What's next for me?" Hatch changed the subject. "What are you going to do? Take me out in the middle of the desert and shoot me?"

"No," Gibbons said. "Like I said, there are people who are very interested in you."

"Interested in me?"

"Call it collectors' art. They found your feistiness entertaining and they already have a buyer."

"A buyer?"

"He's not alone. There will be more who are interested. See, you're up for auction. Don't worry. It'll be an entertaining show. I'm sure you'll give whoever purchases you one hell of a fight, but we are going to make sure that when we deliver you, a package, you'll be in a much more conditioned state of mind."

Drugs. Had she already been drugged? She felt off. Lighter, woozy, but she thought it could have been from the cane strikes. Regardless of the dizziness, she still had enough of her wits to keep up. And she wanted to make sure it stayed that way.

"Oh, and don't worry about those gunshots you fired. The walls are soundproof. This motel may look like a run-down piece of crap, but we have taken precautions." Gibbons rubbed his nicotine-stained fingers together. His pale face crinkled as a smile formed. "It's a big day for us here at the Sunnyside. We've got four packages heading south."

Freddy, the bearded gorilla, turned his bulk to the door and opened it. The headlights of the dark colored van filled the room. She couldn't see the driver, but assumed it was the clean-cut man she'd shot with the blanks. He was the only member of their crew not currently present in the room. Hatch still had no idea where Kaitlin Moss was located.

"Don't bother putting up a fight. You might feel a little dizzy. That's not from the cane. I gave you a little something to calm down. It won't take you completely out of it because I can't have you comatose when we cross the Devil's Pass."

"The Devil's Pass?" Hatch asked.

"It's what we call the waterway that loops between the U.S. border and Mexico. Right here in good ole Nogales. And don't worry, I'll reconnect you with Kaitlin Moss. That's what you wanted, right? You wanted to find her, be her savior? Well, you're going to get to do just that." He pointed at Freddy. "Get her up."

Freddy crossed the room and threw the blonde-haired girl over his shoulder like a sack of potatoes. He disappeared into the light and reemerged a minute later. This time he gripped Hatch by her elbows. "Just give me reason to snap your neck," he whispered. His fiery breath stung her nostrils as he yanked her up. The teeth of the handcuffs ratcheted tighter, biting into her skin around the bones of her wrist.

Hatch kicked out as hard as she could when she stood, crashing her foot down against the bearded man's ankle. He screamed in pain and instinctually reached down toward the source. Hatch followed by driving her right knee into the side of his head, the same side that she had bashed with the Glock. He fell to the side, his skull missing the corner of the end table by a centimeter or two.

Hatch moved swiftly, trying to capitalize on this momentous shift. But Gibbons was already in motion. With no hands to deflect the blow, she tried ducking. This time, instead of a cane, Gibbons brought the butt of his gun crashing down on the top of her forehead. A searing pain accompanied the loud crack. Blood filled Hatch's vision as the light from the van was consumed by darkness.

TWENTY-TWO

A GRAY FLICKERING gave way to clarity. Her face was pressed against the hard liner of the van. In her hazy awaking, Hatch felt every bump of the roadway. Her arms were still clasped behind her and her shoulders ached. The pain in her wrists was nothing compared to the throbbing intensity resonating in her head as she twisted her body into a seated position.

Each time her eyes opened, an intense pain accompanied the effort, causing glimmering stars to fill her field of vision. It was ten times worse than any hangover she had ever experienced, but Hatch was accustomed to pain and worked to overcome this as she'd done several times in her past. The pain radiated from the top and side of where the cane and butt of the gun had impacted.

She tasted blood. She licked her lips, loosening the crust of it from the corners of her mouth. No lights were on and the rear of the van was isolated from the driver's front compartment by a thick black steel wall. In the hazy dark, she ran her fingers along her belt line and felt the raised lip of where she had taped down a handcuff key. Her saving grace. They still had not found it.

She started to fish it out when she heard a scraping sound on the bench beside her. She looked over and she saw the blonde-haired girl from the bathroom seated nearby.

"Are you okay?" the girl whispered.

"Yeah, I think so," Hatch said. The pounding of her head worsened with each word she projected. Even using a whisper caused excruciating pain. The slightest reverberation made her skull ache more. "I'm here to help."

"I can see that." A voice laced with sarcasm sounded from the other side of the van. "Didn't go as planned, did it?"

Hatch's eyes navigated the limited ambient light of the rear compartment and saw another girl seated on the bench across from her. Any hopes the voice came from Kaitlin Moss were dashed when she saw the red hair. Hatch worked herself from the floorboard to the bench seat behind her and took up a spot next to the blonde teen.

The redhead looked angry. Hatch felt the girl's eyes boring into her soul and realized her anger was directed toward Hatch.

"How long have you two been missing?"

"A day. Maybe two. You've been out for a while," the blonde said. "I'm Liz Perkins. Her name's Angela Rothman."

"Liz, you said I was unconscious for a while. How long's a while?"

"I don't know. I was pretty messed up, but I'm feeling better now. If I had to guess, maybe a half hour. I was at that motel for maybe six hours before you showed up."

"You two need to shut up," Angela hissed in an angry whisper. "Shut up or they'll hear."

Hatch looked at the steel barrier sealing them off from the front of the van. Gibbons mentioned the walls of the sleazy motel being soundproofed. It was probable they would take similar precautions in any transport vehicle. Plus, the rumble of the road would muffle anything they said. "We're fine as long as we keep to a whisper."

"Whatever, but you won't like it if they stop and come back here." Angela lifted her hands up to show they were cuff-free. "You see? They like me because I do what I'm told. They won't like you because you don't listen."

Hatch knew why the girl wasn't cuffed. She'd been in captivity too long. Whatever they'd done to her since her abduction distorted the young redhead's perception of reality. A textbook case of Stockholm Syndrome.

Hatch now knew the girl could not be trusted. Her allegiance would lie with her abductors, and right now Angela was complicit in their direction.

The clouds surrounding Hatch's vision cleared, allowing her to view the entire interior of the van. On Angela's bench closest to the rear double doors—what Hatch first thought to be a pile of blankets—was a person.

"Is that Kaitlin Moss?" Hatch asked Liz.

"Figures. You weren't here to save us. It was always about the princess?" Angela shifted in her seat so she was now directly across from Liz. "See? What did I tell you? Nobody was ever coming for us."

"I'm here now," Hatch said. "And I can help. Now tell me, is that Kaitlin Moss?"

"Yes," Liz answered.

"Why'd you call her the princess?" Hatch asked.

Angela sat back. Her red hair fell loosely over her folded arms.

"She calls her that because they've been treating Kaitlin extra special," Liz said.

"How so?"

"Like, she doesn't get touched!" Angela spat the words.

Hatch ignored Angela for the moment. "Is she okay?"

Liz's blonde hair bobbed up and down. "She didn't look hurt, but they gave her drugs. She's been asleep since they loaded us in the van."

Hatch did the math. When she and Gibbons were conducting surveillance, there were three rooms with lights on at the motel. She realized only now that Gibbons had intentionally misdirected her to the wrong room.

"Kaitlin?" Hatch whispered.

"Shh." Angela waved her hands as if trying to block the sound of

Hatch's voice from reaching the unconscious girl. "I told you, shut your mouth."

Hatch stifled the growing anger toward the young woman. "Kaitlin Moss?"

Kaitlin's head jostled and then perked up like a dog hearing a passing school bus.

"Kaitlin Moss?" Hatch said again. This time, the girl slowly pushed herself up using her elbows. Hatch heard the girl's shackles rattle against the bench.

"You?" she said, as if coming out of a dream state. "I... I saw you at the gas station. How?"

Hatch watched the girl strain to make the mental calculation. "I got your message. The pin you dropped."

Kaitlin's body trembled. Tears fell down her face.

"I'm here to get you out."

"What about me?" Liz asked.

"I'm going to get all of you out."

"You're going to get us all killed is what you're going to do," Angela blurted, making no effort to maintain a whisper. "They're not going to hurt us. You are."

Hatch ignored her and focused on the two clearheaded girls. She hoped Angela would listen to what she had to tell them and that some word or other would resonate.

"Your mom is looking for you and I'm trying to help her."

Kaitlin Moss wiped her face on her knees and looked at Hatch again as if for the first time. "You did all this to save me?"

"I did, and I'd do it again if I had to."

"What'd you do, really? Except get captured just like the rest of us," Angela muttered.

Hatch focused on Kaitlin's tear-stained face. "I'm going to bring you home to her. That much, I promise."

"How?" Kaitlin's voice matched her delicate features.

"I have a plan. It's not gonna be easy to pull off. I'm still a little woozy from whatever they gave me."

"And you've got that nasty gash on your head," Liz added.

"I'll be fine. We need to focus on what we know so we can best prepare for the next step. Did you hear anything spoken amongst the kidnappers?"

"Like what?" Kaitlin asked.

"Maybe where we're going or who they plan to meet?"

Liz shrugged and Angela remained closed off.

"Gibbons mentioned The Devil's Pass, a crossover to Mexico. Did you hear anything related to that?" Hatch asked.

"Just that they had to find another way around because of the fire. Not sure what fire they were talking about."

"They talked about a big wildfire on the radio when we were heading down to the motel. I guess it's still not contained."

"They're going to hear you and whatever you think you can do to them, you can't," Angela shouted. "Believe me, I tried. So, either keep your mouth shut or I'm going to come over there and shut it for you. Do you understand me?"

"These are bad people. I know you've been through some horrible things, but I am going to get you out of here, too." Hatch softened the annoyance in her voice. The girl wasn't in control. "Don't do anything that's going to stop me from doing what I need to do if we have any chance of getting out of here. Do not get in my way. Do you understand me?"

Angela looked unimpressed, but Hatch could see it was all for show.

"Just sit there and keep quiet," Hatch said. "You don't have to do anything but that. Can you handle sitting over there like you are doing right now?"

Angela didn't answer.

The rumble quieted as the van slowed to a stop. Hatch sensed a door slam from the front passenger side, leaving her precious seconds to prepare for whatever was coming next.

TWENTY-THREE

"WHAT ARE YOU GOING TO DO?" Liz asked Hatch. Kaitlin slid away from the rear doors of the van, moving closer to the uncuffed Angela.

"I'm going to do what I do best," Hatch said.

"Who do you think you are, Wonder Woman? Who talks like that?" Angela remained in the same position she'd been in for the past several minutes, sitting with her arms folded tightly across her chest. Though since the vehicle stopped, she nervously rocked back and forth.

"Shut up," Liz hissed, "she's here to help. I don't understand why that's so hard for you. She seems like the best chance we've got right now."

Hatch appreciated the teen's misguided attempt at support, but the effort was wasted on Angela. Whatever had been done to Angela's psyche during her captivity would take years for a professional psychologist to undo, or at the very least to give her the coping mechanisms to deal with the trauma. Anything done now to mitigate her allegiance to the kidnappers would be a temporary Band-Aid on a much larger wound.

Liz's comment only fueled Angela's annoyance at Hatch and her desire to escape. "I already told you, you're going to get us killed, lady," she muttered through gritted teeth. Her comment was barely audible as she tried to convince herself.

Hatch didn't engage with the girl. She returned her focus to the rear door of the van while keeping her in mind as a potential X-factor.

A key clanged noisily against the rear door's lock. Her seconds were up. Hatch had hoped to have more time to formulate a solid plan. With experience as her teacher, the best laid plans often went to garbage and the best operators adapted on the fly. Hatch was adapting to the rapidly changing opportunity presenting itself. She couldn't wait for the next chance because the next chance might never come.

"What's she going to do, anyway? She's handcuffed like the rest of us—I mean, rest of you." Angela unfolded her arms and waved her unshackled wrists in the group's collective face.

Hatch worked her fingers between the space between her pants and belt, finding the duct tape's frayed edge. A second later, the small handcuff key balanced precariously in her right hand. Using her pinky finger, she ran it along the face of the cuff in search of the keyhole. Finding it, Hatch awkwardly twisted her wrist and guided the key inside just as the rear door swung open.

The orange hue of the burning Arizona skyline flooded the compartment housing the three teens and Hatch. Freddy, the bearded gorilla, partially blocked out the light. His features were more menacing when accented by the eerie glow.

The big kidnapper's face looked freakish. In the interim since Hatch had last confronted the man, he'd attempted to clean off the blood. But the damage from her blows had swollen his face to cartoonish proportions. His right eye was nearly closed completely, and the blood-soaked bandage across his nose was in desperate need of changing.

"All right ladies, this is the end of the line."

Amid the acrid smell of the burning landscape, Hatch heard the rush of water in the background. *We must be near the waterway they'd talked about. The Devil's Pass.*

"On your feet," he ordered.

Angela was the first to stand. She eyed Hatch warily. Hatch felt the girl's eyes upon her but chose to, once again, ignore her. Hatch focused the brunt of her attention on the man in the doorway and the freedom that lay beyond.

As bizarre as it seemed, Hatch understood Angela's conditioned response. In the big kidnapper, she saw a chance of hope, survival, even if it meant unthinkable atrocities. Life trumped death, and when faced with those two options, human nature sought life. With the order received, Angela was already moving toward the door.

Liz recoiled at the sight of the kidnapper and scooted close to Hatch, bumping up against her and nearly causing Hatch to drop the handcuff key. Hatch could feel the blonde teen's body shake as it pressed tight to her.

The outside air smelled like a fire pit. The wildfire caused by the burning man was apparently still raging out of control in the dry climate. That burning would have been a major draw of police resources.

The oversized kidnapper looked surprised to see Hatch awake and alert. Whatever detour the fires had created in navigating their way down to The Devil's Pass had taken longer than planned. Whatever they'd dosed Hatch with had worn off. With each passing minute, Hatch became stronger and more clear-headed. The decision left was a simple one.

Kill or be killed.

"Hurry up, that fire's going to cut our path off to the river and we need to get there ASAP." He spoke as if his plans mattered to them.

Angela was already standing at the back lip of the open door.

"Get those asses moving!" he yelled.

He reached out his hand. Angela took it. With prince-like chivalry, he guided her down to the road. Freddy smacked her bottom as she slipped beside him. She didn't flinch at the unwanted contact. She did the opposite, offering a smile in return. Hatch watched the girl play the odds in hopes of winning favor.

The gorilla tugged at Kaitlin's ankle. "Time to go!" He released his grip and eyed the teen while patting Angela's head like an obedient dog. "It's a lot easier if I don't have to drag you."

Kaitlin looked to Hatch, her eyes pleading.

"She can't help you. She couldn't even help herself." He laughed.

Hatch swallowed hard, but the words she wanted to offer in response stuck in her craw. The only solace came from her knowledge that action spoke louder than words. She dismissed Kaitlin's non-verbal request for help and kept her mind clear for the moments ahead.

The cuffs clanged noisily against the floorboard of the van as Kaitlin slunk off the bench. She did a modified crabwalk, edging herself forward. With her legs now dangling in the orange light, the large thug reached in and effortlessly hoisted her out. She took a position alongside Angela. Back lit by the firelight, Hatch couldn't see the details of Kaitlin Moss' silhouetted face. But she knew it held complete fear.

Liz was almost sitting on top of Hatch's thigh now. The trembling of her body rattled her cuffs like the chattering of teeth.

"It's going to be okay. I promise," Hatch whispered in the girl's ear.

"No time for chit chat ladies. Move!" He slammed the meaty heel of his palm into the open door to his left, the gong punctuating his intensity.

Liz reached her hands back, squeezing Hatch's knee in a silent goodbye before sliding toward the door. The clattering noise of her cuffs helped to mask Hatch's own noise as she manipulated the universal handcuff key. She twisted the circular end until she felt the ratchet's release. Tension fell away as her left hand came free.

Liz was now sitting on the edge, just as Kaitlin had been moments before. The gorilla's large, velour-covered arms reached up to retrieve her. Hatch exploded from the bench seat. With the cuff still attached to her right wrist, Hatch gripped the open cuff in her scarred right hand with the grooved single strand ratcheted end sticking out like a raptor's claw.

The big man shoved hard at the teen in front of him, trying to clear a path to deal with the unexpected attack. His efforts were foolhardy at best. He should've stepped back to give distance to the charge. But Hatch banked on the large man's lack of foresight. With his hands outstretched after knocking Liz to the side, he'd left himself exposed.

Hatch crossed the six feet of space between them with cougar-like speed. His eyes went wide upon seeing her unbound hands and the silver hook in her right. For all the fear he'd instilled in these girls and the countless others who came before, Hatch was happy to give him a taste of the same. Though his fear was to be short-lived.

His left arm shot out in a desperate effort to deflect the descending strike, but he wasn't quick enough. She slammed the hooked claw into the left side of the oversized trafficker's neck. The metal sunk in deep, penetrating three inches into his neck and only coming to a stop when her fisted grip impacted the moist flesh underneath his dark beard.

His eyes shot wide open and the arm he'd attempted to use to block the blow was now reaching toward his throat. With the cuff hammered into his neck, Hatch kicked downward, stomping the center of his chest above the sternum. The impact forced him back as Hatch pulled the clawed end of the cuff toward her. A sickening sound followed as the cuff tore out a chunk of his throat, severing both his carotid artery and jugular.

His thick beard shielded Hatch from the blood as it sprayed out. He staggered toward the two girls standing nearby. Liz screamed. Angela stood frozen. The arterial spray from his neck lessened with each pump of his fading heartbeat.

He looked around wildly and dropped to his knees. Hatch hopped out of the van and onto the asphalt below as the big man collapsed forward. Liz followed. All four stood by in silence as the dying man's agonal gasps subsided. In it, Hatch could hear his blood sizzling against the hot Arizona asphalt.

She didn't waste time explaining herself to the shocked teens. Liz's scream had undoubtedly alerted the driver. Hatch's suspicion was confirmed when the driver's door slammed.

"Stop messing around with the girls, Freddy. Ghost is going to have your ass in a minute if he finds you're messing with the merchandise before final shipment," the clean-cut kidnapper could be heard saying as he casually approached.

Complacency led to opportunity. Hatch seizing hers, she pounced down on the dying man and searched him, finding a gun and a cellphone. She pocketed the phone and gripped the compact Glock 23 .40 caliber weapon he'd had tucked in the drawstring waistband of his tracksuit pants. The surrounding blood mixed with the ground, matching the maroon of his outfit.

She gripped the gun tightly in her left hand while the cuff dangled loosely from her other wrist. Press checking the weapon, Hatch had to trust this one wasn't loaded with blanks as she took up a shooting stance.

Playing the law of averages, Hatch was poised facing the driver's side of the van. She edged back to get a better angle, corralling the teens behind her. Angela remained rigid, offering passive resistance to Hatch's effort.

Hatch centered her point of aim at the middle of the open rear door of the van just as the clean-cut kidnapper's left foot came into view underneath. She took the slack out of the trigger in anticipation of his next step when she was blinded by an approaching vehicle. She noticed headlights were coming straight toward her. She couldn't see the face of the driver, but she already knew who it was.

The rusted Jeep Wrangler skidded to a stop ten feet from Hatch and the dead man in front of her. Hatch turned and blindly fired twice into the windshield where Gibbons should be. She couldn't see if she'd hit her mark, but she had temporarily halted him.

She redirected her attention back to where the clean-cut man had been standing. His foot was no longer visible beneath the door. The door to the Jeep opened. Hatch turned to see Gibbons' shadowed form back lit against the apricot sky.

Hatch pulled the trigger just as she was struck from the side. The impact caught her off-guard, and she stumbled into the metal paneling of the open van door to her right. Hatch banged her head, reinjuring the cane wound Gibbons had gifted her with.

A fresh trickle of blood overcoated the crust already caked into her matted hair. Hatch turned, expecting to see the clean-cut man's tan face, but was surprised to see Angela instead.

Hatch darted forward and slammed her forehead into the side of the girl's neck, dropping her to ground and rendering her unconscious. Hatch understood the shocked confusion etched into the faces of the two blonde girls standing behind Angela.

A burst of gunshots rang out from Gibbons' direction. Two came close to striking Hatch, plinking the van instead. She fired two more rounds in his direction, shattering the driver's side window. She caught a glimpse of him diving out of the way and toward the back of his Jeep.

Hatch grabbed Angela under her arms and lifted her. She got the teen's limp body into the back of the van before Liz and Kaitlin jumped in to help. Hatch quickly undid Liz's cuffs. "Put these on her."

The girl didn't argue, hopping into the back of the van to do as Hatch directed. The girl's eyes went wide when Hatch started closing the back doors to the van.

"Keep an eye on her. I'm getting us out of here!" Hatch slammed the door and grabbed Kaitlin by the shoulder and positioned her behind.

"Stay behind me," Hatch commanded and then pressed forward to the passenger side of the vehicle with the Glock leading the way.

No sign of the driver. Hatch ducked low and Kaitlin mirrored her. She stayed beneath window level as she moved forward to the passenger side wheel well. She paused beside the wheel. The heated rubber mixed with the noxious odor of the idling engine and wildfire smoke settling in the air around her and left a terrible taste in her mouth.

Hatch heard the shuffling of feet and stood, pressing out with the Glock as she moved. The clean-cut man crossed her sights for a split second as he darted from his hiding spot behind the wheel opposite of Hatch. She fired as he ran.

Even though the three rounds she'd fired didn't hit him, they had given way to another opportunity. One that Hatch seized now.

The driver sprinted towards Gibbons' Jeep. In doing so, he provided Hatch a human shield. "Get in!" Hatch shouted at Kaitlin. She did so without hesitation.

Hatch sprinted around the front of the van and jumped into the driver's seat. The blood-covered handcuff banged against the plastic face of the stereo as she dropped the manual transmission into gear.

Hatch whipped a U-turn, not knowing where she was but knowing enough to head in the opposite direction of The Devil's Pass. Gunfire hit the side panel as Hatch sped by Gibbons. She hoped it hadn't hit the girls in the back, but they'd have to be in a safe place before she could check. And right now, they were anywhere but.

The van raced away with Hatch at the helm as the firelit sky grew brighter ahead. Hatch looked in the side mirror and saw Gibbons racing to catch up.

TWENTY-FOUR

HATCH PRESSED THE MAGAZINE RELEASE, dropping it on her lap as she continued to drive with the gas pedal floored. She eyed the back of the mag and did a quick count. Four rounds in the magazine. One in the chamber, a total of five rounds of 180-grain Smith & Wesson hollow point. She reseated the magazine in place and gave it an extra tap for good measure. Hatch tucked the gun to the small of her back and looked at the scared girl in the passenger seat, hoping it would be enough.

Hatch uncuffed herself, letting the cuffs drop to the floorboard. Kaitlin faced away from her, exposing the keyholes toward Hatch. A couple seconds later, the girl's wrists were free.

"What's the plan, now?" Kaitlin asked.

"See if you can get his phone open." Hatch pulled the phone out from her pocket and handed it to Kaitlin. She figured any teen had a better chance of figuring it out than Hatch.

Kaitlin Moss's face was cast in the screen's glow a moment later. "What should I be looking for?"

"Check the text messages. Maybe there's info on the route so we can be sure to avoid it."

Kaitlin tapped the screen a few times and scrolled the display. Hatch saw her face drain.

"What is it?"

Kaitlin took a second before answering while continuing to stare at the screen in disbelief. "My father. Well, stepfather's number is right there."

"What did it say?"

"The last message reads: Notify me when the package is sent." Kaitlin's voice was absent of any emotion. "The message was sent two hours ago, but I don't understand. Why would he be involved? Was he trying to buy me back in a ransom deal? Or..."

Hatch was quick to understand. Kyle Moss had sold his daughter into sexual slavery. She didn't want to confirm the girl's suspicion, so she answered Kaitlin's unasked question with a dismissive statement geared at refocusing the girl to their current situation and away from the why. "Right now, all that matters is the two major problems right in front of us."

"And what are those?"

"The guys with the guns behind us, and the wildfire ahead."

They crested a small rise in the road. Off in the distance, the landscape burned bright as the fire's wall spread out as far as they could see.

Kaitlin used the dead man's phone's GPS to map a route from where they were back to Nogales, which wasn't too far from their current location. The problem was getting there. The fire line extended across every roadway in their immediate area. The wildfire was spreading rapidly, isolating Nogales from the rest of the world. Hatch took things off-road.

The van banged and dipped and swayed and bounced along over the uneven, unpaved dirt trail she was following.

"Wouldn't the cops be able to help us?" Kaitlin called out over the clamor.

"They're most likely tied up by that fire or cut off from us by it." What Hatch wanted to say was that she didn't trust anybody else right now. She then thought better of deceiving the girl and followed with, "And after what Gibbons pulled, and the lack of help from the detective working the case, and your father's potential connection to all this, I'd rather trust in myself."

Kaitlin drummed her fingers.

"I'm going to get you home, Kaitlin. That's one thing I can promise."

Kaitlin was quiet and looked out the window, avoiding eye-contact with Hatch when the dead man's cell phone rang. The screen's display showed the caller id belonged to Ghost. Hatch took it from Kaitlin and answered.

"Just pull over and drop the girl. We only want Kaitlin." Colton Gibbons' raspy voice filled Hatch's ear. She wanted to reach through the digital space connecting them and crush the face of the man holding the cell phone on the other end.

He was playing with her. Hatch played along. Every minute spent talking meant a minute he wouldn't try to shoot. She needed to buy time until she saw an opportunity around the wildfire's line.

"You'll just kill us when we stop." Not that she was considering stopping.

"Listen, we'll back off. Give you a safe distance to release her."

"Trade me for them," Hatch countered.

Gibbons laughed. "Hey listen. I'm all for picking a more ripened apple, but our buyers have very particular tastes. Sorry, as attractive as you may be, you do not fetch the same price and that is not an offer we're willing to accept."

"I don't think you see my potential," Hatch said.

"Oh, I do. What I also see is that my early retirement bonus is sitting right next to you, and I need to get her where she belongs."

"I'm doing that right now. She belongs with her mother."

"I'm telling you, you can walk away a hero. The lady who rescued two girls from a human trafficking ring. Just leave us Moss within the next mile and you'll be a headline hero by morning."

Hatch ended the call. She had a mile to decide her next move. At the speed she was going, the timeline was fast approaching, but so was her opportunity.

Hatch couldn't go around the wildfire, so she decided to go through it.

Colton Gibbons was closing in behind her and time ticked down. She thought about brake-checking them in the doubtful hope it would send them into a spin.

The flames burned bright as Hatch barreled ahead toward a water refinery plant. Steam billowed out, smudging the pastel sky. Steam could mean the fire had met with the water reserve or the water lines branching out beneath the ground.

A moment later, Hatch had her answer.

An underground water line had ruptured. The endless gallons of water bubbling forth had, if only temporarily, cut a swath through the fire. The gap created was just wide enough for the van to squeeze through.

Hatch jerked the wheel to the left at the last second, turning toward the steaming hole. A risky move considering the van's top-heavy stature. But it worked. The Wrangler skidded sideways. As Gibbons righted his Jeep, Hatch saw another pair of headlights approaching. She'd assumed it was coming but was surprised the backup hadn't arrived sooner. Hatch figured when the girls didn't make their next waypoint, backup had been called in.

Kaitlin must've seen a trace of worry cross Hatch's face. "What are you going to do now?"

"I'm going to keep my promise." If she were to shake the tail completely, she would have to make sure there was no tail left.

At all.

TWENTY-FIVE

HATCH ENTERED the tunnel of fire. An oppressive swelter consumed the interior of the van. She worried about the safety of the two girls trapped in the rear. Sweat soaked her skin in a glimmering sheen. Fire licked at the exterior. The glow against her skin reminded her of the day she'd received her scar, and, like the fire raging out of control around her, her determination to survive this encounter burned as brightly. If not more so.

"They're gaining on us," Kaitlin called out. She was keeping rear guard as they drove through the heated path.

"I guess they're crazy enough to follow us," Hatch muttered.

The flames were close, but the water flowing out from the underground piping was keeping them at bay. For now, at least. The ground burned like ripe coals in a grill. Hatch had brought them halfway through the flaming corridor. If they stopped here, they'd be in their own personal hell. One hundred feet further, and they'd be on the other side of the wall. Closer to freedom. There, she'd have more ways to navigate away from Gibbons and the other vehicle pursuing close behind.

The van's front right tire blew first, immediately followed by the left rear. It threw the van violently from side to side as the heated ground cooked the rubber of the tires. A deafening screeching sound of metal on metal filled the air when the exposed rims scraped across the broken pipe.

Hatch fought to control the van, righting it as best she could. They were almost sideways now as they approached the end of the firebreak. When the third tire blew on the back right, the back end dragged. The van was barely plodding forward. The heat intensified as their pace slowed. Hatch wiped a thick layer of sweat from her brow.

Gibbons slammed the front end of his Wrangler into the back of the van. Just like the deceptive man who drove it, the Jeep had a lot more under the hood than its outer shell showed. Hatch launched the van through the last few feet of the fire into the open air. The last tire exploded. The vehicle swerved to a stop. Hatch gave one last ditch effort to get the van moving but abandoned the idea almost as soon she started. They were trapped, and that left her only one option. Fight. With three scared teenagers and five bullets, Hatch didn't like the odds. But in her life, the odds were always stacked against her.

The van's final resting place left it angled with the driver's side away from where Gibbons' Wrangler and the accompanying blacked out SUV were fanned out on the other side.

"Just like before. You stay on my six. Right behind me, Kaitlin."

"Are we going to be okay?" Kaitlin Moss' voice was soft and made more angelic by its juxtaposition to their current circumstance.

"I need you to be my shadow. Do you understand what I mean by that?"

Kaitlin looked terrified. Hatch wasn't sure if she should leave her.

"If I move, you move. Tell me honestly, can you do that?" Hatch paused for a moment to allow the traumatized teen to process. "Otherwise, I'm going to have to come back for you."

Kaitlin nodded. "I'm ready."

Hatch pulled her shirt collar up over her face to use as an improvised mask, making her look like a convenience store robber. Kaitlin mirrored her as they both slipped out the driver's side door. The mask did little to aide against the acrid air swirling around them.

Hatch stayed low and so did her shadow. They left a few inches gap, ensuring the hot metal of the van's exterior didn't contact their skin.

"We've got to get the girls out of the back," Kaitlin said, the shirt muffling her voice.

"I know. The heat could kill them. But there's no chance of getting that rear door open without dealing with Gibbons and his men first." Hatch thought for a moment about what she was about to ask the girl. It was the best option out of a pile of bad plans. And that was all Hatch needed. "How good are your acting skills?"

"Played a tree in my third-grade performance of Romeo and Juliet. Does that count?"

Hatch laughed and felt relieved at the teen's resiliency. "I need you to walk to the rear with your hands up. I need you to surrender yourself to Gibbons."

"Wait. What? No way I'm turning myself over to them!" Kaitlin was almost shouting. "Please, I'll fight! Just tell me how."

"You're not understanding me. I'm not giving you over to them. But I need them to believe that I am."

"How do you plan to do that?" Kaitlin said. "You just drove through a wildfire to get away. They will not believe you suddenly gave up."

"True. But if they believe I'm unconscious, they might." Hatch ran her fingers along the blood-soaked hair and smudged them across her face. "That'll make it look good when they come for me."

"Are you sure this will work?"

"No," Hatch answered. "But we're running out of time, and this is the best option I've got."

"If I do this, it's going to get me back home to my mom?"

"It's our best hope of making that happen."

"Then what are we waiting for?"

Hatch laid herself down on the ground. It was warm, but not in the same ballpark as the scalding coals in the passage through hell they'd navigated. Sprawled out on her back, she kicked her left foot up onto the bottom lip of the opened driver's side door. It would hopefully give her the appearance of collapsing out of the vehicle. This gave her easier access to the Glock concealed along the small of her back.

The web of her left hand was seated into the curved tang of the pistol's grip. She closed her eyes after Kaitlin disappeared out of view around the backend of the van.

"She's dead or seriously injured." Kaitlin called out. "Somebody's gotta help her."

Hatch listened to the conviction in the girl's voice. The throatiness of the choked back tears helped nail the performance. Hatch was confident they'd buy it. A temporary silence followed. Gibbons was taking precautions it wasn't an ambush.

He broke the quiet and began commanding the girl. Gibbons ordered Kaitlin to open the rear door. The door banged open and Hatch could hear two sets of feet hit the ground. Hatch was happy to learn both girls were still alive, even if their condition was unknown to her.

The girls were marched away. Their footsteps faded and were replaced by the fire dancing nearby. With her eyes closed, Hatch slowed her heart rate and focused on the sounds around.

Four seconds in.
Hold.
Four seconds out.
Hold.
Repeat.

She waited as the fire's glow penetrated her closed eyelids until she heard footsteps.

The other men chasing them must've been busy reacquiring the girls into their custody because Hatch identified one set of feet approaching. She hoped it was Gibbons. Her left index finger rested on the outside of the trigger, waiting to be called to service.

The feet were close, almost on top of her. Hatch waited, then heard the shuffle of feet. She opened her eyes just in time to see the bottom of a size twelve boot hurtling toward her head.

Hatch rolled into the other leg and locked his shin against her collar bone. She scooped his ankle with her right hand. In a push-pull movement, Hatch swept the planted leg. The move tossed him backward before the right foot collided with her head.

Hatch maintained control of the man's leg and crawled across his body, mounting his chest and trapping his left arm. It was not Gibbons or the clean-cut man. She realized this killer must've come from the SUV. He maintained his weapon during the fall and was bringing it up at Hatch's midsection.

She rolled sideways to the right and fired her weapon, putting two rounds in the side of his chest cavity with the third striking the side of his head near the ear. The rounds contorted the man's body. His weapon skittered across the ground several feet from Hatch and landed halfway between where she was now kneeling and the rear of the van.

Hatch had two rounds left in her Glock and there were at least two more men she had to deal with. She moved low and fast toward the gun in the dirt. Two feet from the dead man's weapon, she was greeted by the clean-cut kidnapper's tan face. He looked half as surprised as Hatch to see her alive. In that fraction of a second's distraction, Hatch seized the opportunity to dive backward toward the front of the van.

She rolled as soon as she hit the ground. She found protection behind the van's engine block as a hail of bullets peppered the hood.

With two rounds remaining, Hatch prepared to make her final stand. In the back of her mind, doubt crept in. "She's going to get us all killed," Hatch heard Angela's voice from earlier. She hoped she didn't prove the fiery teen right.

TWENTY-SIX

HATCH POISED herself in front of the van's front grill. It had been less than a minute since the last gunshot, but time stood still. Nobody had come for her yet. Maybe they wouldn't come at all? Hatch worried she might've turned the girls over to the people she'd promised to protect them from.

The last grains of sand hit the bottom of the hourglass. The waiting game was over. If she had any chance of saving the girls, the time was now. Her skull continued to throb. She broke cover as the familiar scratch of Colton Gibbon's voice cut the silence.

"You know how this story's going to end. You either toss the gun where I can see it and walk out from behind that van," Gibbons coughed. "Or you die, here and now."

Gibbons made a critical error in his attempt at a barter. Hatch didn't have any plans of surrendering. And now she pinpointed his location.

Hatch pushed herself outward from around the corner of the van, letting the green glow of the night sights guide her like a lantern. Her target, the pale head of Gibbons, peeked out from between the Jeep and the SUV. The headlights' intersecting cones of light partially hid him, but the fire back lit him.

Hatch took aim as the pad of her finger found the trigger. Before she could pull the trigger, a flash of light seared her vision erasing Gibbons from view.

The wind shifted, redirecting the path of the fire. A line of dancing flames sprinted through the gap, creating a fiery barrier separating Hatch from Gibbons, separating them by a blast of fire two feet wide and about ten high.

Through the flickering fire, Hatch caught sight of Gibbons helping the clean-cut gunman shove Kaitlin Moss into the back of the SUV. Hatch took aim on the moving targets, trying to get a clear shot without the teen in the backdrop.

Kaitlin fought back, swinging her arms and legs wildly about. As the two traffickers battled for control, Liz launched out like a blitzing linebacker slamming into the quarterback. Her body crashed into Gibbons, knocking him backward as she landed on the ground.

Gibbons recovered and rushed into the fray. He picked up Liz and dragged her back to the SUV's open rear door. Hatch didn't have a kill shot, but she had a debilitating one. She pulled the trigger, sending a bullet down range.

The hollow point found its mark, slamming into Gibbons' left hip. The impact buckled him, folding him in half before sending him spiraling to the ground. Liz ran to the far side of the Wrangler.

Kaitlin broke free and joined in the hasty retreat.

Gibbons lay bleeding but was alive, clear from his effort to try to scoot behind the SUV. His clean-cut partner rushed to his side and attempted to render aid.

Hatch now had both men free and clear in her sights but had one shot to take. She weighed her decision in a millisecond. The tipping point was Gibbons' veiled threat about Hawk's Landing and Savage. It would eventually lead to her family. The image of Colton Gibbons anywhere near Daphne sickened Hatch. The burden of decision was made easy by the man's very existence.

Hatch fired her last round. The Glock's slide locked to the rear as

Hatch looked down the end of it and saw the gaping wound in the center of his pale skull. She'd killed the Ghost.

The last man standing looked over toward where the girls had run. He then frantically scanned for the shooter. Even through the flames, she could see the death of Gibbons shook him.

Her weapon was empty. But he didn't know that. She dropped the magazine on the ground near her boot. She then thumbed the slide release, bringing it forward and making it look like it was still in battery.

The fire taunted her, reminding her of that day overseas. The memory tingled her arm and unlocked her fear, sending her heart to the races. Her chest tightened as her lungs fought to extract oxygen from the smoky air. She remembered her father's timeless lesson about the true definition of bravery, *"...is found not in the person who is fearless, but in the one who recognizes fear and chooses to face it head on."* Hatch's next decision would prove once and for all which category she fell into.

Then she did something she never thought she'd do in a million lifetimes. Rachel Hatch, survivor of an IED blast, ran through the wall of fire.

Hatch shielded her face with her arm as she broke through to the other side. She smelled the singed hair. Her clothing was on fire and she dropped into a modified combat roll, dousing it.

Hatch raised her empty gun, same as she would've had it been loaded, and pointed it at the clean-cut trafficker's head. Whether she'd gotten the drop on him or if it was the sight of the crazy woman running through a wall of fire, Hatch would never know. But without firing a shot, he slammed the back door of the SUV closed and ran around to the driver's side.

The SUV kicked dust and debris in Hatch's direction as it fishtailed a turn and drove away. The brake lights disappeared into the tunnel of fire surrounding the fire break.

The size of the break caused by the water pipes began to shrink. The encroaching flames were swallowing the steam.

Hatch ran over and traded guns with the dead Gibbons, leaving him with the empty weapon responsible for the dead trafficker on the other side of the van. That'd be a mess for the police to sort out after an anonymous tip.

"Girls? I'm coming around to you," Hatch announced, not wanting to surprise the jumpy teens.

She walked around the Jeep to find both girls cowering together. Kaitlin was gently caressing Liz's hair as she stared blankly at Hatch. "You came back for us."

"I made you a promise."

Hatch helped them to their feet. It took a second before she realized Angela was missing. "Where's Angela?"

They both pointed in the direction the SUV had just departed.

"Get in, " Hatch called out as she jumped into the Wrangler. The keys were in the ignition and the motor was running.

Kaitlin climbed into the passenger seat and Liz filled the back. Hatch turned to give chase.

"Where are you going?" Liz cried.

"I can't let them take her." Hatch understood the concern. The teen would have to understand her need to disregard it.

Hatch turned the Jeep around. As she raced forward, she saw the fleeing SUV safely navigate the firebreak seconds before the fire completely overpowered the water's resistance. The wall of flames closed them off from Angela.

Sitting in the dank, cigarette-filled Wrangler, Hatch silently vowed that once these two girls were safely returned home, she wouldn't rest until she found Angela Rothman.

With burdensome regret, Hatch brought the Wrangler back around. She sped off into the night, leaving the sight of their standoff to be ravaged by the wildfire. Hatch set out to fulfill a promise to a mother to bring her daughter home.

TWENTY-SEVEN

HATCH DROVE ALONG IN SILENCE, giving the two girls accompanying her time to process that they had escaped from Gibbons and his men. She kept her gaze on the rearview mirror, but since driving away from the wildfire burning a path across Nogales, there'd been no sign of any pursuing vehicles. Hatch attributed part of this to her belief it would be unlikely Gibbons, in his role as Ghost, would have had a transponder attached to his Jeep. He was a man who purposely shielded himself from others. She assumed the same would be true with his employer.

Even though the wildfire had almost killed them, it also played a role in their ability to escape. The wall of flames continued to serve as an impassable roadblock. Hatch feared the fiery gate would only hold back the traffickers for so long before search parties would try to hunt them down. But the wall of fire had disappeared completely from view thirty minutes ago. The orange glow behind them held its last vestiges as Hatch raced north into the darkness ahead.

"I'm sorry," Kaitlin said. It was the first word's she'd spoken since getting into the Wrangler. "I forgot the phone. When the van crashed, I must've dropped it. In the chaos after, I totally forgot to grab it."

"No need to be sorry," Hatch offered.

"It had my stepfather's number. It had the information proving he was involved with this." The mention of it almost caused Kaitlin to break down in tears.

Hatch pulled out a cellphone from her pocket. "It's okay. I've got his." In her hand was Gibbons' phone. She'd grabbed it when she traded guns with the dead man.

Kaitlin shuddered and released the tension in her shoulders.

"You did great back there." Hatch looked in the rearview mirror at Liz laying half-dozed in a fetal position on the worn fabric of the backseat. "Both of you did."

"Thanks," Kaitlin whispered. Hatch saw the girl's mouth move but, even though they were now traveling on paved roads, the *whomp-whomp* rumble of the Jeep's knobby tires drowned her out.

"That was real hero stuff back there, girls. I wouldn't have been able to do what I did had it not been for you two."

Hatch saw her cellphone stuffed in the cupholder next to a half-empty pack of Marlboro Reds. She reached down and picked it up. Limited service. The prepaid plan she'd purchased promised unlimited coverage. The bars on the display said otherwise. Hatch tried anyway, dialing the number and pressing the green call button. Willow Moss answered before the first digital ring completed its song.

"Hatch?" Willow's groggy voice came through choppily.

Hearing Willow use Hatch's real name caught her off-guard, but she rebounded in under a second, remembering she had been the one who told her while they sat outside her childhood home. "It's me."

"Please, God, tell me you found her?"

"I have somebody here who wants to talk to you." She could hear Willow Moss suck in deeply and hold her breath. Hatch then handed the phone over to her daughter, seated in the passenger seat.

"Momma," Kaitlin's voice squeaked. Both mother and daughter openly wept for an inconsolable minute. Hatch didn't interrupt the reunion. The tearful sobs heard over the roar of the engine brought memories of Daphne and Jake to the forefront of Hatch's mind.

The tears slowed as Kaitlin regained composure. "I'm coming home, mom." Her voice cracked, a combination of dehydration and smoke inhalation. "I love you," she said, before handing the phone back to Hatch.

Hatch cradled it against her ear as she drove. She squeezed the wheel tightly to keep the Jeep's vibrations from shaking the phone loose.

"Thank you!" Willow screeched.

"I don't make promises often. But when I do, I make sure I keep them."

"Where's Gibbons? Is he okay?"

Hatch heard the concern in her voice. It was genuine. Hatch could tell the desperate mother on the other end had no idea of Colton Gibbons and his involvement with the kidnappers. And that meant she didn't know about her husband's hand in all this.

"He's dead," Hatch flatly stated.

"Dead?"

"Long story. And one that will take time to sort out. Take comfort in knowing Kaitlin is safe. We can talk more when we get there. We're less than an hour out."

A sigh of relief filled the receiver. It sounded as if Willow had been holding her breath for two days since her daughter's abduction and the news of her pending return finally allowed her to release it.

Hatch needed to place another call, but before ending this one, she said, "Is your husband home?"

"Yes. He's in our home office. He's been up all night working on some huge business deal. I mean, how could he care so little?"

Hatch knew exactly the deal he was working on. And she took pleasure knowing the package he sold was being returned to sender by way of a stolen Jeep.

"Why? Do you need me to get him?" Willow continued.

"No. But I need you to do me a favor and tell him absolutely nothing. I'll explain more when we get there."

"Okay." Willow's voice betrayed her discomfort. "I'll be ready."

"See you soon," Hatch said before ending the call.

Kaitlin showed the drain of the past few days. She was left both emotionally and physically depleted from the ordeal. All of them were.

Liz had drifted off to sleep during Kaitlin's brief phone call. Hatch had intended on calling Liz's parents afterward, but, after seeing the sleeping girl curled up in the backseat, she let her rest until they arrived at the Moss estate.

Immediately after Kaitlin spoke to her mom, she had slumped against the window. She was asleep within seconds. Hatch was still riding on the adrenaline rush fueled by the chaos of the previous hours. There would be a time to reset later, as with any battle. A cooling off period to decompress and recharge her batteries would be needed after this was all over, but she wasn't done yet. She wouldn't be done until she had reunited the two girls with their families.

Hatch continued their northerly progression toward Hermosa Valley as the cityscape of downtown Phoenix came into view. She dialed another phone number and waited for it to connect.

Hatch thought about calling Williamson after learning from Gibbons that the Hermosa Valley detective wasn't involved. He was just inept. Willow had explained the childhood friendship of Kyle Moss to the detective, so she decided against it. Her story would be a hard sell for any agency, but harder when the investigating officer was blinded by a personal relationship.

Knowing this, Hatch went outside of Hermosa Valley's jurisdiction. And after a minute of lag time, the Arizona State Police dispatcher had transferred her, connecting her with the on-call Major Crimes detective, Detective Sergeant Cameron Lacey.

"I'm calling you regarding a recent abduction and its connection to a human trafficking ring operating within your state."

"Go on," Lacey said. Even at three in the morning, this detective seemed more engaged and more interested in what Hatch had to say than Detective Williamson had when she'd presented herself at the Hermosa Valley Police Department. Her mind reeled as Hatch absorbed that the chaos she'd endured began with her stop at the Gas-N-Sip less than twenty-four hours ago.

"I have located two missing girls. Three, actually." Hatch thought of

Angela. "Two of the girls are in my care. Their names are Kaitlin Moss and Elizabeth Kennedy."

"You have the Moss girl?" Lacey asked.

"Yes. She and Liz are safe with me."

"And who are you?"

"That's not important." Hatch dismissed his question. "A girl by the name of Angela Rothman is heading south toward the Mexican border. She's in a dark SUV, driven by a clean-cut Hispanic man. They're heading for a place called The Devil's Pass."

"Lived in Arizona my entire life and never heard of any Devil's Pass."

"That's what they call it."

"Who's they?"

"The traffickers. It's what they called the waterway they use to cross the border. It's down by Nogales."

"There's a big wildfire down there right now."

Hatch rubbed at the raised scar tissue of her arm. It still tingled from the fire's heat. "I know. Just send somebody down that way and call Border Patrol. Please."

"Will do. As soon as I finish getting all the information from you."

"There'll be time for that later. Kaitlin and Liz are safe with me. Angela Rothman isn't."

Lacey was silent for a moment, as if weighing the veracity of Hatch's statement before offering a mumbled, "If you say so."

"The Moss case is currently in the hands of a Detective Kevin Williamson out of Hermosa Valley PD."

"Have you already been in contact with him regarding the information you've just provided?"

Hatch needed to approach her next answer carefully. "I have not. With your expansive jurisdiction, you have more resources at your disposal." Hatch left out the part about Williamson's incompetence, but did add, "Plus, there's a conflict of interest."

"And what's that?"

"Williamson is friends with Kyle Moss."

"And what's wrong with that?" Hatch heard a trace of annoyance in the sergeant's response.

Hatch lowered her voice, knowing that Kaitlin was half-asleep but probably listening. "Kyle Moss was directly involved in the kidnapping of his stepdaughter."

The silence that followed spoke of the comment's impact.

"On that front," Hatch continued, "I'm going to need you to meet us at the Moss residence. We're less than twenty minutes out now."

"Okay."

"And there's something else."

"Go on."

"I have one of the abductor's cell phones. I'm sure your digital forensics team can extract valuable information from it."

"Of course. Yeah. We've got a great team here and we should be able to extrapolate if there's good data. I'll see what I can do." He paused. "How'd you come by way of getting that phone and recovering those girls?"

"We can talk about that when I see you."

"Is that it?"

"For now," Hatch said. Then followed with, "I don't know how far this network of traffickers goes. They have money, power, and a lot of reach. That's why I called you. I figured, and I hope to God I'm right, that you guys at the state aren't tied up in this. They seem well-connected in both law enforcement and otherwise, and they have the money to back whatever it is they're doing."

"I get it. This conversation will remain between us and, of course, my partner. I'll keep what you tell me confidential."

"See you at the Moss estate. We can talk about it there." Hatch relayed the address to the detective. "It's a big estate in Hermosa Valley. And just so you know, Willow, Kaitlin's mother had absolutely nothing to do with her daughter's disappearance and was actively seeking her recovery."

"Fair enough."

"I'm sure Kaitlin and the Kennedy girl know enough to help you further your investigation. You're also going to want to check out the Sunnyside Motel in Nogales. It's owned and operated by the traffickers. They use it as a holding area for the girls before they ship them to Mexico."

"Jesus," the detective Sergeant said. "All right. Lemme grab my partner and we'll get out there to meet you as soon as we can. I'm about thirty minutes behind you. I'm coming from home, so I've got to stop in at headquarters and grab a couple of things before I head over. Mark my words, I'll be there."

Hatch hung up the phone.

Kaitlin stirred. "Who was that?" She mumbled as she woke from her dream state.

"State Police. They're going to help set everything right."

Kaitlin rolled back into her nook. The hum of the Jeep Wrangler lulled her back to sleep as Hatch drove the rest of the way to the girl's palatial home.

TWENTY-EIGHT

HATCH PULLED the gunshot riddled Wrangler up to the front gate of the Moss manor. The grinding gears made a loud noise as she slowed to a stop, waking both sleeping girls. Hatch nudged Kaitlin's shoulder. "Hey, you're home."

Kaitlin rubbed her eyes and stretched. She looked at her house from outside its closed wrought-iron gate.

"Don't worry. Arizona state police are on their way. They should be here within the next fifteen minutes." Hatch then looked at the girl in the backseat, who looked in awe at the massive estate illuminated by the coming sunrise. "They're going to get you home too, sweetheart. I promise."

Liz nodded. "You live here?" she asked in a whisper.

Kaitlin gave a modest nod and then shrugged.

Hatch knew her home would feel different now that she knew her father's involvement. Everything would be different. Forever. People always wanted things to go back to what they were. They always wished for the "before a tragedy struck" but wishes and wants were for fairytales. And Rachel Hatch didn't live in a fairytale world.

She was familiar with the cold, hard reality that hardship provided.

The burdens carried only accrue over time and often never lighten. The Wrangler's headlight cast its glow across the black iron bars of the arched gate. Hatch cut the engine and exited.

It felt good to stretch her legs in the cool morning air before the sun positioned itself in the sky above them and began its daily ritual of baking the Arizona ground.

She rubbed at her scar. It seemed fresh again after running through the fire. Like the demonic hold it had over Hatch, it had awoken. It hadn't itched like this in the year since her recovery. But with it, another sensation crept to the surface. An old, familiar one. Hatch had an itch for justice, and she wanted it scratched.

Hatch strode up and pressed the buzzer to the gatehouse. A gruff voice met hers and she immediately recognized it.

"Open the gate." Hatch dismissed any attempt at cordiality.

"The hell with you, lady."

She was happy to hear the tension in his voice and only imagined what he must be thinking. Hatch looked up into the window where she had seen Willow before. She was there again now.

The guard stepped out of his guard house to flex his muscles and try to intimidate her. He looked far less menacing with the white bandage over the broken bridge of his nose. The dark circles of bruises gave his eyes a raccoon-like quality.

"I told you, you ain't getting in here, lady."

Hatch thumbed in the direction of the girl in the passenger seat. The guard looked wide eyed at her as Kaitlin and Liz stepped out from the Wrangler.

"Open the gate," Kaitlin snapped at the guard.

He retreated to the guard house and a moment later an electronic buzzing accompanied the squeak of metal as it opened wide.

Hatch entered with Kaitlin and Liz at her side. The guard recoiled in fear.

Kaitlin noticed the damage to his face. "What happened to you, Teddy? Looks like you got hit by a bus."

He didn't answer.

Hatch continued walking, following the landscaped path leading to the main doors.

"Seriously, what happened to him?" Kaitlin asked Hatch in a whisper.

"He tried to stop me from speaking with your mom."

"Doesn't look like he made the right decision." Kaitlin gave Hatch a tired smile.

"He won't have to worry about that much longer. I think your mom is going to be making some changes." Hatch winked.

The front door opened, and Willow stood in the threshold wearing a lightweight nightgown draped over her slender frame. Kaitlin darted up the steps. Her mother met her halfway. The two embraced, tears streaming down both women's beautiful faces. Willow buried her head into the neck of her daughter and inhaled deeply, as if trying to breathe in her very essence. Hatch stood by, absorbing the moment. It reminded her of leaving Hawk's Landing. She remembered her last kiss goodbye to Daphne and Jake. And of course, Savage.

Willow looked over at Hatch after releasing her daughter from a tight hug. She mouthed the words, "Thank you."

Hatch looked at Willow and noticed the slight shiner under her left eye. She had tried to hide the bruise. The coverup would've worked from a distance. But up close, it was impossible not to notice. It confirmed what Hatch had suspected early on, that it wasn't just psychological abuse.

Not only had Kyle Moss sold his daughter into slavery, but he had also abused his wife and forced her into another form of captivity. Even surrounded by the ornate home and spacious grounds, the Moss estate was a prison. All of it sat poorly with Hatch. To what end had Kyle Moss entered the arrangement to sell off his child, Hatch didn't know, nor did she much care. There'd be no reason or explanation to validate it.

"Where is he?" she said.

Willow looked scared. "Upstairs, in his office. He's been on the phone all night, screaming, yelling. I've never seen him this frantic before."

Hatch had a good idea why. "Point me the way."

"Is that a good idea?" Willow's hand trembled.

"It won't take long. Just point me the way," Hatch said.

"What happened to Gibbons?" Willow asked.

"He's dead," Hatch said.

"You told me that, but how?"

"Mom," Kaitlin interrupted. "He tried to kill us."

Willow looked aghast as she placed her hand over her heart.

"All of that will be explained when the state police arrive. And I don't want to be here when they do," Hatch added.

"Why? Didn't you tell the police you'd meet them here?" Willow asked.

"Better I'm not around. Trust me."

"I do." She kissed the top of her daughter's head. "You brought my baby girl home."

"How do I get to his office?" Hatch asked again not masking her annoyance at the passing seconds.

Willow Moss turned and led them inside. "Follow me."

She led Hatch up the stairs. A custom designed kachina-stained lead glass chandelier hung from the vaulted ceiling. Hatch traced her fingers over the braided copper railing as she traversed the hand-crafted tile inlaid stairs.

Willow brought them to a set of copper doors. They were closed, but she could hear a man inside stringing together a series of expletives capable of making a sailor blush.

"I'm going to need a few minutes alone. Is that okay?"

"Are you going to kill him?" Willow asked with no hint of sarcasm.

"I'm not planning on it," Hatch answered honestly.

Willow had a seriousness in her eyes. "You take as long as you please," she said through gritted teeth.

The hate that Willow kept locked inside was presenting itself. Hatch guessed the woman's story and could only imagine how deep that hatred went for the man who'd abused her over the past fifteen years. She no longer attempted to shield her daughter from the gritty truth that was her life.

Hatch stood in the hallway and took a second to listen through frosted glass encased in etched bronze.

"I don't know what happened. You gotta believe me. I had nothing to do with this. I honored my end. You can't do this to me. I'll be crippled. Do you understand? This was my chance to pull us out. This was going to give us the money we needed to reset things, to bring the business out of bankruptcy."

Hatch opened the door and stepped inside.

Kyle Moss was fit and attractive, belying the darkness that lay beneath the polished surface of his manicured image. He looked at Hatch in confusion. "Who the hell are you?"

Hatch shut the door behind her. "Hang up the phone, Kyle. We need to talk, and I need your undivided attention."

"This is my house, you crazy bitch!"

Hatch walked over and backhanded the millionaire, slapping the phone from his hand. Her scar burned. The impact knocked him into the plush leather of the seat he was standing beside. All his fancy degrees and pictures with dignitaries scattered across the wall couldn't change the fact he was looking up into the cold, dead eyes of somebody who wasn't fooled by any of it.

"Your conversation is over." She kicked his right ankle, preventing him from rising. "And ours is about to begin."

"What the hell? Do you know who I was talking to?"

"Does it look like I give a damn?"

As powerful as the man was in business, realization washed over his face that it had no influence over Hatch. She moved closer. He cowered and raised his hand to protect himself should another backhand be on deck.

"Here's how this is going to go." She pulled the gun she'd stolen from Gibbons and pressed it against the cheek she'd slapped. "The only thing stopping me from killing you right now is that girl outside. She's seen enough death to last her a lifetime. All that came because of what you did."

"I didn't—"

She slapped him with the pistol. Not hard enough to do damage, but enough to shut him up. "Don't waste another breath trying to convince me. There'll be plenty of time for that when the Arizona State Police arrive." Hatch cast her eyes at the fancy clock on the wall behind him. "And they're about ten minutes behind me."

"State Police?"

"Yeah. Looks like your buddy Williamson is going to get a little boost to his subpar investigative skills."

Moss quivered and pressed himself into the couch to separate himself from the muzzle pressing hard against his cheek. He seemed to come around on who was in charge now.

"Ten minutes from now, your entire world will be turned upside down." Hatch's finger tapped the outside of the trigger housing. "I have a right mind to put a bullet in your head, but your life can be better served in other ways. The hell that's coming for you and the time you're going to spend in prison will have to suffice."

"Prison?"

"You didn't think you could buy your way out of this, did you?"

He didn't answer.

"You can't. Not this time. Nobody is going to look the other way on this."

"And why's that?" It was the first attempt at resistance offered since the slap, but it came across as weakness.

"Because you're going to talk. You're going to tell the investigators everything they need."

"And why the hell would I do that? I've got the best lawyers money can buy."

"They can't stop a bullet."

Hatch looked at the ticking clock and stepped back, tucking the Glock into her waistband as she did so. Moss collapsed his face into his hands. She half-thought he was about to break down in tears.

"If you don't do the right thing, if you don't tell the authorities every detail about who's involved and how this operation works, you'll be seeing me again. The knowledge you have is the only thing keeping you alive."

He dropped his hands and locked eyes with Hatch. "Please don't do this."

"I don't deal with people who hurt the innocent. I punish them." Hatch took a step toward the door. "I have people, too. Very connected people. Connected in many different ways. If I hear from them and find out you didn't do your part, you'll be in a world of hell unlike any you've ever known. I will come back for you. There's no place on this earth that you could hide from me. And there isn't a legal system in the world that can protect you from what I am going to bring upon you."

"Christ lady, who are you?"

"It doesn't matter who I am. I don't exist. And if you ever see me again after this moment, you're already dead." Hatch let the words hang in the air for a second and watched his eyes water as he choked down the message. She read his body language. Everything she saw led her to believe he would do as he was told. Life trumped death. Even a life spent in prison.

"Please, don't do this."

Hatch scoffed. "It's already done. I've done nothing but clean up the mess you created. I told you what you need to do. Any deviation from that is a guaranteed early visit to the grave."

Hatch turned away without giving him a second thought.

Willow was still standing down the hallway, near her bedroom, with Kaitlin and Liz beside her. Hatch walked up. "You're safe now. Detective Sergeant Lacey from the State Police should be here any minute."

"Aren't you going to stay? You look like you need medical attention. Can I get you something? Can I pay you? What can I do?" Willow asked.

"You can take care of your little girl and make sure that bastard in there never, ever touches you or her again."

Willow nodded. "What about you?"

"I've gotta go."

"But I don't understand?"

Hatch handed over Gibbons' cell phone. "Kaitlin knows enough to help ensure Lacey has a good starting point. He knows what to do with this cell phone. Just make sure he gets it."

"I will."

"This has the data that the state police will need to track down the people who did this to your daughter, and so many other girls. It's the beginning of what will be an awfully long investigation. But I'm hoping that my instinct is right and that Sergeant Lacey's gonna take care of this for you. I'll have somebody check in on the case from time to time, to make sure that everything is working in your favor."

Hatch turned to leave. Her time on the grounds of the Moss estate had to reach an end if she had any chance of departing before the cavalry's arrival.

Kaitlin ran to Hatch. So did Liz. They both latched onto her in a tight embrace. Hatch awkwardly tried to refuse it at first, but then accepted the contact. She put a gentle arm around each of them, her scarred and damaged arm pulling Kaitlin Moss close.

"Listen, girls. Don't let the horrors of what happened to you define you. Use it as fuel. Learn from it. Be stronger because of it."

Hatch then separated herself from the girls and slipped down the hallway, down the stairs, and out the door. She passed by the guardhouse. Teddy remained inside with the door closed as Hatch walked out to the rusted Jeep Wrangler.

Camelback Mountain filled her rearview as she drove the stolen Jeep back to where she had parked her rental car.

After taking a few minutes to sanitize the Jeep of any evidence of her presence, Hatch got into the Ford.

She drove away from the coffee shop where she'd first met Gibbons and headed south. She had a promise to keep. And out there was a redheaded girl secretly waiting for her to make good on it.

.

TWENTY-NINE

AFTER GIBBONS and the tall woman with the scarred arm had left, Alejandro Dominguez had spent nearly an hour inside the abandoned desert warehouse struggling to bring his cuffed hands in front of him. He'd ended up having to slip off his shoes to give him the extra wiggle room to bring his hands through underneath his lower body. In the effort, his right shoulder popped out of socket. It still ached, and it had been over twelve hours since they'd departed.

How long was Gibbons going to leave him here? He knew that the man they called The Ghost worked in unusual ways. His methods of carrying out his business had always fascinated Dominguez. Being on the receiving end of it left him feeling what others must've felt. Terrified.

Dominguez remembered the shock of seeing Gibbons after the fender bender. But then the woman from the gas station was there. It didn't make sense to him then, and still didn't. Then Gibbons chased him down and brought him here. He thought it was an execution. Dominguez recalled his fear while standing outside the door to this abandoned building.

But it wasn't an execution, it was an interrogation. Dominguez didn't know what to do when Gibbons started asking about the operation. What kind of game were they playing? He knew better than to talk. It was why they'd hired him. He didn't talk to cops. But it wasn't the cops, it was Gibbons.

It took him a couple of minutes for his nerves to settle before he realized that Gibbons had been guiding him forward. He told him about the girl because that's what Ghost wanted. Then they left. Dominguez still had no confirmation if he'd passed whatever test he'd been given. Whoever that woman had been, she had Gibbons jumping through hoops.

Day had given way to night, and Dominguez had given up hope. He ventured out from the confines of the warehouse and confirmed what they'd told him hadn't been a lie. He was in the middle of nowhere. Dominguez walked for twenty minutes and saw no sign of life. Not wanting to chance his luck with wild animals, he retreated to where he'd been waiting.

Whatever Gibbons was doing, it appeared Gibbons had forgotten about him. Dominguez' stomach rumbled loudly in the quiet of the large, hollow building. He tried to sleep but couldn't. Every time his eyes closed, he'd hear noises, none of which were man made.

The Arizona heat of day escaped through the broken windows scattered along the faded walls was now replaced by the cool night air. A chill settled into his bones, causing Dominguez to shiver. He tucked himself in a corner of the room. The wall retained some of the day's heat and he pressed against it, absorbing as much of it as he could. He rocked back and forth in a seated fetal position and waited for the next day to break. He'd try to make another attempt at walking his way back to civilization then.

He heard it before he saw it. The sound carried across the barren wasteland. A car was fast approaching. Gold slivers cut through the darkness around him as the headlight's beams wormed their way through the cracks in the wall. Dominguez' body went rigid. He stood and pressed himself flat against the wall.

Dominguez was weaponless and handcuffed. He had to make a conscious effort to breathe. He inhaled the musty air and waited.

The vehicle came to a stop. The engine was still running when he heard the slam of a car door. He edged himself along the wall until he found a fractured seam and peered out. The headlights blinded him and the only thing he could make out was the shadow of a person rapidly approaching the front door. His heart was in his throat as he braced for the entrance.

Light flooded the dark interior of the abandoned warehouse as the front door banged open. Dominguez was frozen.

"Alejandro?" It was a woman's voice.

He squinted against the light as her features came into view. A feeling of relief washed over him. "Cassandra? Is that you?"

She turned to face him. Her long dark hair fell across her perfectly sculpted shoulders. Dominguez fought the urge to run to her. Keeping his cool, he forced a casual strut as he crossed the concrete floor to the woman whom he secretly desired.

"Thank God you're here." He tried to not sound too desperate but wasn't confident he'd nailed it. "When the Ghost left, I didn't know what to do."

"You look like hell." Her face was welcoming. It was no surprise she was so effective at recruiting the young girls.

Dominguez shrugged awkwardly. "Been a long night."

She sniffed the air. "Smells like piss."

Dominguez was embarrassed and wished he could retreat to the dark to hide the redness filling his tan cheeks.

"Let's get you out of those cuffs." She moved in close.

The smell of her fragrant perfume pushed back against the dankness he'd suffered in over the past twelve hours. Dominguez bathed himself in it as he extended his arms. "I can't tell you how happy I am to hear that."

A second later, the cuffs released. Dominguez immediately nursed his wrists. They'd been rubbed raw in several places. Regardless of the current pain, the relief of having them off outweighed any discomfort.

"Thank you. For a moment I believed you were here to kill me."

Cassandra gave a smile. Her beauty would rival that of the legendary Helen of Troy. "Now, why would you think that?"

"I don't know. Figured I screwed up." Dominguez looked away from her. "That lady, the one with The Ghost, she saw me. Figured that's all she wrote for me."

Just then a second car door banged shut from outside. A moment later, Trevor Fairmount entered and took up alongside Cassandra. Dominguez wanted to punch the skinny man in his throat. He'd been the one who said they should stop at the Gas-N-Sip. It was his idea to let her use the bathroom. Dominguez seethed as he contemplated all he'd endured because of that stupid choice. He wanted to knock the smug look off his bony partner's face.

"Look at you pretty boy." He mussed Dominguez' hair. "Rough night?"

Dominguez bit his lip. It was all he could do to keep from pouncing on the man. "Shut your stupid mouth." The words came out in a low growl.

"Boys, let's not get our panties in a bunch." Cassandra stepped back a few feet from both men. She pulled a silenced pistol from the small of her back. "You both screwed up. And now you both have to pay for it."

The first shot passed through the right side of Trevor Fairmount's skull out his left temple, showering Dominguez in blood and brain matter. He threw his hands up and dropped to his knees as the gun's barrel turned his way. "Wait! Please! I did what Gibbons wanted! I did what he told me to do. I only said the things he wanted me to. Just call him!"

"Who do you think gave me the order?" Cassandra winked.

Cassandra's serene smile was the last image Dominguez had before the bullet penetrated his brain.

THIRTY

THE PHONE only rang one time before the person on the other end picked up. "Hello?" His voice seemed to melt the cold hardness around her heart. Just hearing it in the one word he'd spoken brought Hatch back. It hadn't been that long, but it might as well have been a lifetime since they'd seen each other. As things stood now, it could be a lifetime before they ever did again.

"Hello?" he asked again, not recognizing the number she was calling from. "I can hear you breathing, so speak your peace or I'm hanging up."

"Dalton." The silence from his end of the phone was as if the phone had cut out altogether.

"Hatch?" He asked.

She changed out the SIM card on her new phone regularly, but she still felt that all it would take was for Talon Executive Services people to tap in or put in a remote receiver designed to pick up certain transmissions. Would they devote that much time at verifying if she were still alive? She hoped not, but she needed to maintain that level of vigilance until she confirmed otherwise. If not for her, then for the people she loved. And this call was a risk, but a risk that was balanced by need. "I'm in a bit of trouble. Well, I was. Not so much now. But I'm sure I will be again soon."

"Are you okay? Tell me where you're at and I'll come for you." Savage was alert now, the grogginess dissipating completely.

She knew what he said was true. If she asked, Dalton Savage would already be in a truck, driving her way.

"I can't ask you to do that," Hatch said.

"You've got me worried. What's going on?"

"I've come across kids being trafficked."

"Can't you go anywhere without trouble finding you? I mean, what's the point of leaving here if everywhere you're going creates a fireball of chaos?"

He didn't know how accurate his word choice was in relation to what had just happened.

"Listen, don't worry about me. I'm fine. And I don't pick the fights, they pick me. When they do, I can't walk away."

"I know. It's what I love about you."

Love. The word punched Hatch in the gut. She pushed it from her mind. "There's some girls in a lot of trouble right now. I crossed paths with an ex-cop who wasn't playing for the right team."

"What happened?"

"It's complicated."

He seemed to understand what she was hinting at. Hatch thought back to Gibbons from his first impression to his last. She couldn't believe she had trusted that he was a comparable second place to the man on the phone. Even though he was now dead, Hatch couldn't let go of the fact she'd fallen prey to his deception.

"This group running the girls, they're a bad news operation all the way around. Not that any of them are good, but this one, this one takes the cake. It's more complex than anything I've seen in my investigative time."

"What do you want me to do?" She loved that Savage asked. No judgment, no advice, no guidance. Maybe he had learned in their time together that it was a waste of breath to provide any of those. That Hatch would have already decided. And that it was better to support her than to get in her way. Or maybe it was just in Savage's nature to always do the right thing. It was what drew her to him in the first place. A purity of kindness lay inside the hardened exterior of the licorice-eating sheriff.

"I reached out to the Arizona State Police. A Detective Sergeant Cameron Lacey from their investigative Bureau is handling it now. I just want to make sure that everything works out. I want to ensure that the people responsible are punished accordingly."

"Where the hell are you right now?" he asked.

"I'm outside of Phoenix."

"Okay. Shouldn't take me but a half day's drive. I can be there within six, seven hours."

"You're not understanding me. I don't need you to come here. It wouldn't matter if you did. Because I won't be here when you do."

"What do you mean?"

"I've got somewhere else to be. I can't monitor this thing and verify it the way you can. I'm going to send you the contact information for Lacey when we hang up. You can reach out any way you feel comfortable. Maybe make it look like you're looking into a case, I don't know, you're a smart guy. You'll come up with something. I just want to make sure the Moss family is taken care of. In particular, the daughter Kaitlin and her mother Willow. Kyle Moss should be spilling his pathetic guts to the investigators as we speak. Please ensure it's a detailed retelling that exposes his involvement. If not, I've got some unwanted cleanup to handle."

"Okay. I can do that." He paused a beat. "And then how do I get in touch with you?"

"You won't be able to, but I'll reach out to you. Promise." She winced after uttering the word.

"What's the other thing?"

She always liked that Savage could read between the lines when paying attention. It was an endearing quality of his.

"Make sure I'm clean. I was using a pseudonym. I tried to cover my tracks, but I screwed up. I'm not sure who knows I'm here. I'm not sure how compromised I may be. But when you pry into the case, find out what they know about me, if anything at all."

"And if there is?"

"We'll cross that bridge when we get to it."

"Fair enough," he said.

Hatch was happy to have the business end of the call completed. "I've been pondering a way to stay connected to the kids. I'm lost right now. I hate not being there. I hate not being there for them."

"I was over there this morning." Savage said. "I can't help myself now, I feel responsible."

Hatch was as jealous as she was grateful.

"They're going to grow up fast," he said.

Hatch had the same gut-wrenching sensation as when she watched them walk away, fleeing her childhood home as the flames engulfed it. "I miss them terribly."

"Daphne lost a tooth today. She's proud of herself and wrote a nice big letter to the tooth fairy."

Hatch smiled and had an idea. "Maybe I'll be her tooth fairy."

"What?" Savage chuckled at the comment. It only took a matter of minutes before they settled back into the comfort of their relationship. Now completely severed and fractured by Hatch's death, albeit a fake one.

"I'm sorry," Savage said. "I'm having trouble picturing you in that role. Maybe if you were the one knocking teeth out."

She laughed softly. The ringing in her head continued, serving as a reminder of the damage she'd taken at the hand of Gibbons. "You said she wrote a letter, right?"

"I did."

"Well, the Tooth Fairy's got to write back."

"She'll love it," he said.

"I can use it as a secret way to communicate with them to keep me alive in their minds. I can't let them go."

"Hatch, you never have to worry, the bond you have is forever forged and can't be broken—"

"I know," Hatch said, interrupting.

But there was a truth in his words. The passage of time did amazing things in the augmentation of trauma and happiness. It could erase pain and heal wounds, both external and internal. But time also erased memories. The longer she remained disconnected from her home, the harder it was for her to access those memories. And for the kids, they would fade even faster.

Returning after her fifteen-year absence had been a powerful, overwhelming experience that had released a flood of memories she had either repressed or lost in the shuffle of life. She didn't want that to happen with her niece and nephew, with her mother, with Savage.

Maybe her interim job as tooth fairy correspondence expert would assist her in maintaining that connection a little longer until she could figure out a way back home. The only way that could happen was if she could be free of her past. It's the only way she could keep her family safe.

Right now, she had to worry about keeping another person safe. That person was likely through The Devil's Pass and trapped in a hellish nightmare south of the border.

"If you're not sticking around Arizona, do you mind telling me where you are off to now?" Savage asked.

"If I tell you..."

"I know," he said. "I get it. Then I become a potential liability."

"Right," Hatch said. "Sorry, I just can't do that to you."

"I understand."

Hatch felt the need to give Savage more. He deserved it. "I couldn't save one of the girls."

"I'm sure you did your best. We can't save them all," Savage offered.

"I made a promise to her. And now I have to bring her home."

"I feel sorry for whoever gets in your way."

"Me too," Hatch said. "Me too."

Before clicking off the phone, before saying goodbye yet again to the licorice-eating small-town sheriff who'd won over Hatchet's heart, she managed to say, "I miss you, Dalton."

"Every day," was his simple but powerful response.

Hatch ended the call. She sat for a few moments fading into the song playing. An update on the car radio broke her trance. The wildfire was being contained. They had reestablished road access to Nogales. Good news for Hatch as she drove south.

She had another detour before making her way to California.

Another promise to keep.

Read on for a sneak peak at Whitewater (Rachel Hatch Book Six), or pre-order your copy now:

https://www.amazon.com/gp/product/B08P27ZT4P

BE *the first to receive Rachel Hatch updates. Sign up here:*

https://ltryan.com/hatch-updates

WHITEWATER (SAMPLE)
RACHEL HATCH BOOK SIX

by L.T. Ryan & Brian Shea

Copyright © 2020 by L.T. Ryan, Liquid Mind Media, LLC, & Brian Christopher Shea. All rights reserved. No part of this publication may be copied, reproduced in any format, by any means, electronic or otherwise, without prior consent from the copyright owner and publisher of this book. This is a work of fiction. All characters, names, places and events are the product of the author's imagination or used fictitiously.

WHITEWATER: CHAPTER ONE

"You know I honor family above all else? For me, there is no greater priority. Our family is stronger than any other. The reason for this is simple. We built it brick by brick through blood, sweat, and tears. The toils my father endured not only put us in our current position, but they set the example we all follow. It made each member of the family strong. But as with any foundation, the family is only as strong as the sum of its parts."

Raphael Fuentes stood in the corner of the room and listened as his father, Hector, delivered his ceremonious speech. It wasn't the first time he'd heard it, or at least a variation of it. The man had raised Raphael. And over his twenty-three years of life, he'd listened to his father espouse the meaning of family, and its worth. He'd grown up loving Hector, not just for the power he wielded, but for the love he had shown Raphael and his two younger brothers, Gabriel, Jesus, and in the last three months, Guadalupe.

He could see that his father hadn't been as pleased when his sister had been born. Hector wanted only boys. As a child, Raphael knew his father's love was genuine, but doubted his sister would ever come to know it. His father didn't give his love freely. It came at a hefty price, its tolls increasing with each passing year. As the oldest male heir to his father's fortune and power, Raphael learned at an early age what it meant to rule and lead as his father had. At seven years old, Raphael had watched his father use a dull machete to execute a man who had wronged him.

Even witnessing the beheading and the many following in its wake, Raphael went to bed every night praying for the strength to be his father, to walk in the man's gigantic footsteps. And every morning when he woke, Raphael was saddened to see he was still the same. He did his best to prove himself worthy. By the age of thirteen, Raphael realized the differences between his father and himself spread as wide and long as the Rio Grande River, cutting its path outside his hometown of Juarez. As Raphael matured, his father took him to places he'd never been, showed him things he'd never imagined, and taught him what the family business was really about.

Raphael felt a disconnect upon learning the true source of his father's power and influence. Afterwards, Raphael felt like he had never known the man at all. He saw it in his father's eyes too, the darkening. Over time Raphael's displeasure grew obvious, and his father had begun to question whether Raphael was fit to lead and thus was putting on such a big show. It was another lesson, another opportunity to test whether Raphael had proved his worth.

"But even the smallest fracture in any foundation can lead to bigger cracks until it all crumbles down." Hector Fuentes instructed the room's attendees including Raphael, who remained silent while his father addressed the group. No one interrupted Hector Fuentes without consequences. Depending on their status within the family, certain consequences had life-altering repercussions.

"What we do here matters. What we say to others matters. The money, the power, it means nothing if we don't have family. If I cannot trust every member in this room to carry forward the ideals and the secrets that our family holds, then it is all for naught. That's why today saddens me as much as it angers me."

Seated in the center of the room sat a woman bound to a chair. Thick plastic zip ties held her ankles and wrists in place. A rope wrapped around her midline under her ample breasts, sealing her to the back of the chair.

Hector reached down and grabbed the top of the hood shrouding the woman's face and head and ripped it off. Raphael's eyes moistened at the sight of his mother's tear-soaked face. Raphael did not make eye contact with her. He couldn't afford to let his father see the pain in his eyes and the hate that would surely follow. Raphael looked just to the side of her at the hulking shoulders of a mountainous man. His father's right-hand security man, Edgar Munoz.

Munoz did a stint in the military before returning home to serve as Hector's most trusted soldier. He stood by with his gold deadpan eyes and scanned the crowd. Even in the close circle of friends, family, and upper echelon of the Fuentes Cartel, his father was smart enough to know that threats could come from anywhere. The woman bound to the chair was a testament to that.

Hector worked the room, moving around and making eye contact with each member present as if he were a politician at a speaking engagement. "Isabella, my love, to see you sitting here, tears at my soul." The words sounded genuine, and maybe at some point they would've been. The words might still hold some truth of the love Hector and Isabella had once shared. But loyalty trumped all else, including love.

To Raphael, his father's words sounded rehearsed. His father did everything to perfection. That's why Hector dished out repercussions when his meticulous plans went awry.

"But you betrayed me." Hector turned and bent down, bringing his face inches from his wife's.

"Please," she uttered, barely above a whisper. Her voice quivered. She choked it down like an overcooked piece of steak. Then came a flash of defiance in her deep-set eyes. This resistance only seemed to energize Hector's fervor.

He stepped back and panned out to the audience. "I loved her. I still love her. She is the mother of my children and gave birth not three months ago to my daughter, Guadalupe. Your sons stand by and watch." His voice darkened. "Because of what you did, they have to suffer.

Because of what you did, our family must suffer. There is no worse crime than turning on your family." Raphael heard his father's words and recognized the hypocritical connotation.

"Please," Isabella Fuentes sobbed. "I did it for—"

"Save your breath," he barked. A froth of spit came out of his father's mouth, in contrast to his normally reserved demeanor. He was enraged and nearly launched at her. "Not only did you go behind my back, you went to the police. The police! There's no reason you could give to ever justify what you did. But just like a crack in any foundation, if it's addressed early enough, it can be patched up. It can be repaired. And that is what I'm going to do here now. The police officers you spoke with have already been dealt with. There's just one more small crack that needs filling."

"No," she whimpered. Isabella fought to turn her head around, twisting it, craning her neck to look at her first-born son.

Raphael could no longer avoid eye contact. He met his mother's tearful eyes, and the sight of it nearly broke him. He bit the inside of his lip so hard he could taste his own blood. She pleaded with him without uttering a sound. Her silent cry for help tore at his soul.

"You have been called here today to bear witness to this... so no other crack, no other fracture in our foundation, will ever happen again. Remember this moment."

Hector moved quickly. Slipping in behind Isabella, he grabbed her forehead and jerked it back against his chest, breaking her eye contact with Raphael. He looked on as his father ran the sharpened edge of a long-bladed knife across the throat of his mother.

Raphael Fuentes remained motionless as the blood spurted. He listened to the choking gurgles of his mother's dying breaths. He willed himself not to look away as his mother's life slipped from her body.

WHITEWATER: CHAPTER TWO

It was dark, but the sandy ground she laid on still carried the warmth of the day, even though the surrounding air had cooled dramatically in the shift from day to night. A wind had kicked up sand, still carrying remnants of the nearly contained wildfire seven miles from where she now lay. The massive efforts to contain the wildfire had been successful, and they worked now to extinguish remaining embers, but the air continued to reek of its damage. The wildfire had burned in a twenty-mile crescent extending from Nogales. Hatch still felt the memory of its sting.

Ash and soot still drifted like dirty snow, laying a thin coat over Hatch during her seven hours of waiting. She welcomed the gray camouflage now covering her body. She'd returned to the area in which the traffickers had taken the girl without knowing where The Devil's Pass was located. She had traveled the same road where the first gunfight with Colton Gibbons and his fellow traffickers had taken place. When she passed by the spot, seeing no evidence of the violence from less than a day before surprised her. She stopped and looked for any shell casings. She found none. Even the blood had disappeared. None of the media sources she'd searched had anything about the event. Her trail was clear and as was the traffickers'. She was dealing with a highly organized group of individuals.

It would be only a matter of time until she saw what she was looking for. So, she hunkered down and waited. Patience born by necessity. She skirted the border until coming to an empty swath of open space. There was no way she could enter Mexico legally without a passport or identification. Since she was legally dead, neither one of those things were available. To do it through an alternative channel would take time she didn't have. So she waited.

Hatch lay on the ground seven miles west of the Nogales border crossing. She selected her current location by asking one simple question, where would I try to cross the border? It had taken eight hours before she'd proven her decision right.

She heard it before she could see it. There were no buildings nearby, no streetlights, no lamps or sources of man-made light in sight. The only light provided came through the cloudy ash covering the sky above. To Hatch's benefit, being bathed in the darkness gave her more flexibility in her choice of concealment.

She heard a crunching noise up ahead, followed by the coo of a baby and the mother trying to quiet it. Somebody snapped, yelling in Spanish a phrase Hatch didn't understand, but the tone of which was easily discerned. Anger. The cooing stopped, and the procession continued. They weren't quiet by any stretch, although Hatch could tell they were trying to be.

As they came into view twenty feet from Hatch's position, she counted seven heads: an old man, a pregnant woman with a small child, a young mother carrying a baby, and two men. The older man was heavyset and used a walking stick to navigate the uneven terrain in the dark. He stumbled once, and the younger man at the back of the pack kicked him hard enough for Hatch to hear. The older man grunted softly, and then got back to his feet, offering no form of resistance. The man who had kicked him was their coyote, a paid shepherd of human beings. Most of the people in that group undoubtedly gave their life savings for this journey, or would be indentured upon arrival, possibly for the rest of their lives. Crossing the border from Mexico to the United States, with the hope of a better life was no effortless task. Often, the American Dream was more of a nightmare.

Human trafficking was a modern form of indentured slavery. These people each had a predestined destination, where they would serve out whatever sentence until their debts were paid. Hatch watched as the group came to a stop, now only fifteen feet from where she lay.

Hatch remained tucked tightly to a rock, making herself as small as her 5'10" frame would allow. The large rock aided her ability to mask herself from the headlights of the approaching van. The small boulder shielding Hatch cut the beams in the shadow, keeping her invisible to the man driving. The coyote shoved the other six border crossers in the back of the van. A very brief exchange between the coyote and the driver followed, and within a minute, they were gone.

Hatch remained still. She waited until the van was out of sight. The taillights disappeared as the van crested the small rise in the dune nearby. Twenty seconds later Hatch's night vision returned. The details of her surroundings came back in full view as she watched the man who had just offloaded the six people into the van.

He took a moment to smoke a cigarette. The embers burned, casting him in an orange glow, and blinding him to her movement as she broke cover and stood up. He wasn't looking in her direction and he hadn't turned.

She crept along the dirt and rock, rolling heel to toe on the outside edge of her boot. She moved forward, keeping her knees bent just above a half squat. Like a tiger, she was ready to pounce. She wanted to get close to him before addressing him. Within five feet, he still had not noticed Hatch's presence. She could see now that he was armed. She hadn't expected otherwise. He carried a revolver, a strange weapon for a man in his line of work. With six shots and six people, he could've easily been overwhelmed. But the power of a coyote didn't come with the ammunition in their guns. The power of a coyote came with the influence they had over people's lives. The families left behind could easily be gotten to and harmed. There was power in the control mechanisms beyond that of a one-hundred-eighty grain hollow point, like the bullets in Hatch's gun. She didn't draw it or plan to. She had other plans for the man in front of her.

He blew out a long puff of smoke, and Hatch spoke, "Hola. Cómo estás?" She knew little Spanish but figured it might put him more at ease if she started in his native tongue.

The man spun and reached for his gun.

Hatch threw her hands up. "Wait, wait, wait!"

He paused and looked back toward the massive fence dividing the two countries. He was frantic and looked as though he were about to run. "No policía," she said.

He looked around, expecting to see a hoard of border patrol agents rushing in his direction. But there were none. No car waiting for him outside. Hatch had parked the vehicle she used to get here nearly three miles away. After clearing her DNA from the car, she lit it ablaze and walked the rest of the way.

He was curious now. His hand went off the gun, and he squinted his eyes at her as he took another drag of the cigarette. "What the hell do you want, lady?" he asked in broken English but easy enough for her to understand.

"I don't want any trouble. I just need to get across the border."

"You need to get across the border?" He looked confused. "Why don't you...?"

She knew what he was going to say. "Why would any American citizen need to illegally cross the border to Mexico?" She couldn't give him an answer, but this was a man of secrets, this was a criminal, and her reasons didn't matter. Only one thing mattered to a man like this.

"I've got a thousand dollars. Take me across to Mexico. I'll give you half now and the rest when you get me across." Hatch pulled out an envelope with five hundred dollars inside. She showed it to him but didn't give it to him. Not until he agreed, which he did with a shrug. He stood there and counted it for himself. He flicked the cigarette off into the dry dirt beside him and didn't bother to squash it out. "Get you across the border and there's five hundred more?"

"That's it." She knew he had other plans in mind when they got across, but she'd deal with that when it the time came.

"Nobody smuggles themselves into Mexico. You must be crazy or desperate."

Hatch knew better. She was both.

WHITEWATER: CHAPTER THREE

Hatch followed the coyote through the desolate landscape, moving among the dark shadows. The sure-footedness with which the smuggler navigated the uneven terrain in such limited lighting spoke volumes about the countless times he'd taken this path before. Hatch thought of the innumerable human lives he'd shuttled across this same path. She thought of the suffering this man and men like him had subjected their own people to. Up close and personal, modern day slavery didn't look all that different when compared to smugglers of old in a world with a long and ugly history of this unforgivable abuse.

She despised the man ahead of her. The smell of his stale cigarettes mixed with the funk of his body odor made the already repugnant man even more so. She hated needing his services. She would've favored putting a bullet in the back of his head, but small fish needed to be thrown back. Killing the sour smelling man would do little to help the girl she'd come to save. Missing an opportunity to rescue the feisty redheaded teen, Angela Rothman, had led her here. Hatch couldn't allow her disdain for the coyote leading her to affect her decision to follow. She'd done it countless times before during her time in the military, in particular the years she was assigned to Task Force Banshee, with varying results. Working with indigenous people was the only way to move about in a foreign land. It was one of the Green Berets' specialties and Hatch, being qualified on that front, understood it better than most. Still, she wouldn't hesitate should the smuggler turn on her. But that hadn't happened yet.

Two miles into their trek, light penetrated the high rust covered steel of the twenty-foot high fence separating the United States from Mexico. They were close, just shy of a hundred feet from the border, when the coyote stopped. A gap of five feet separated Hatch from her guide. He turned to face her. Hatch's left hand was already behind her back. The web between her thumb and index finger pressed firmly into the tang of the Glock she'd taken off the dead traffickers in Arizona. The coolness of the steel slide calmed her.

No way he could unholster his six-shooter before Hatch dropped the hammer. In the split-second it would take to end this standoff; Hatch was confident in her probability of victory. But this didn't remove the tension. Maybe it was the calm in his dark eyes that gnawed at her nerves. He looked smug, like he knew something she didn't. Was it a trap? She scanned the periphery and saw no other sign of a threat.

He didn't seem to notice her hand or the intensity in her eyes. Or if he did, he didn't seem to care. "The hard part comes next. If you're ready?"

"Lead on." Hatch's grip on the Glock loosened, but she maintained her position.

The coyote slowly scanned the wall in both directions before squatting by a small rock and shrub. Hatch's eyes tracked his movements. Atop the rock was a coiled rattler. She didn't hear the familiar tat-tat-tat of its tail warning of an impending strike. It didn't react to the coyote's proximity. In that moment, she thought of Dalton Savage, the sheriff of Hawk's Landing who'd given Hatch a new lease on life, and the snake that had nearly ended his.

The smuggler must've seen her reaction to the nearby snake, subtle as it was. His thin-lipped smile exposed yellow stains of the few teeth left in his rotten mouth. "El senuelo."

"No entiendo." Hatch shrugged.

"Decoy." He grabbed the snake and set it on the ground next to him.

Hatch squinted and realized the rattler was a fake, albeit a very realistic one. The coyote then pushed aside the rock. Using his hand, he cleared the dirt and sand, exposing a circular wooden door roughly three feet in diameter. He pulled a long knife from the sheath on his belt and dug the tip into the seam. A few seconds later, the coyote pried it open.

Hatch stepped forward. The hole was pitch black, and the coyote offered no light. She then looked out toward the wall. In that moment, Hatch realized the next hundred feet would make the two miles they'd traversed seem like a walk in the park.

"You first." The coyote gestured his hand toward the hole.

"No." Hatch was poised to strike. Unlike the fake rattler on the ground nearby, her venom came in the form of the match grade ammunition loaded in the semi-automatic pistol tucked in the small of her back.

The crooked smile fell away from the dark-skinned smuggler's face. He was silent for a few tense seconds following Hatch's comment. He shifted on his heels and grunted. He pulled out a cell phone and mashed his weathered fingers onto the buttons of the flip phone before dropping his feet in the hole. He looked like a kid wading into a pool. "Five hundred?"

Hatch slapped the thigh pocket of her tan cargo pants. "It's right here. Just get me across and it's yours."

"Pull it closed."

"What about the rock?"

He tapped the closed cellphone in his hand before returning it to the front pocket of his jeans. "They fix."

The text message she'd just watch him send made sense. A tunnel like this would require a team, not only to build, but also to maintain its secrecy.

"After you." Hatched stepped closer. There was an unfamiliar smell, a worse smell than the coyote emanating from the hole.

No further discourse followed. The tenuous deal had been brokered.

The coyote disappeared, swallowed by the darkness as he dropped into the hole.

Hatch waited for half a minute to avoid piling on top of the smuggler before sliding in feet first as she'd seen him do. With her body halfway in, she grabbed at the wood door and inched it closer so that the outer lip protruded past the hole's edge. Hatch shimmied herself underground. Using her fingertips, she slid the door closed.

The limited ambient light above was now only visible through the imperfect gaps in the wood door's slats as Hatch began working herself deeper into the restrictive space.

Hatch inched downward. The tunnel dropped in at an angle like a crude playground slide. Instead of a smooth ride down, the surface she scraped along was lined with jagged bits of rock poking out from the packed earth. The butt of her Glock banged noisily as she moved deeper. She thought of the challenges faced by the pregnant woman and the woman carrying the baby when navigating their way.

She could hear the coyote ahead but couldn't see him. The soles of her boots hit bottom at twenty feet down. From there, the tunnel leveled out and was slightly larger than the confines of the angled descent. The additional foot of space in the excavated tunnel enabled Hatch to assume a crawl. She edged forward in the dark, her knees banged painfully into the hardpacked dirt while the coyote led the way.

Her right hand pressed on something moist. She didn't need to see to know what it was. Whether the fecal matter was of animal or human origin was debatable. She wiped off the remnants against the dirt wall before continuing.

Hatch kept track of the distance she had traveled by placing her hands tip to palm. Every time her right hand struck the dirt floor, she counted one foot. It was a rough system of estimation, but it helped ease the strain of forging ahead into the unknown. By her assessment of her underground trek, Hatch figured she had just passed the halfway mark.

She banged her head on an unseen object. Hatch ran her hand along the edge of what felt like the edge of a wood support beam. It was splintered at the center. She could still hear the coyote scraping his way along ahead of her. The weight of the ground above had collapsed at some point. Hatch blindly felt her way around the opening.

She pressed her body flat against the dirt and snaked forward in a low crawl. The tunnel walls gripped at her shoulders like a boa constrictor. Each breath filled her mouth with the dust and dirt kicked up from her exertions.

She shifted her torso and hips as she snaked her way for the next ten feet before the tunnel opened back up to its original size. Taking up a crawl, Hatch made up for lost time and quickly caught up with the coyote.

They continued unimpeded until they came upon a slight incline. The coyote stopped and Hatch ran her dirty fingertips into the worn treads of his cowboy boots, nearly jamming her knuckles.

"Just up there." It was the first time she could see his face again as the light above penetrated a seam in another door, this one made of metal instead of wood.

He crawled up the rest of the way to the door and banged twice on its metal exterior. After the long silence, the noise was deafening. A few seconds later, a metal latch releasing signified the message had been received.

A hinge barked its request for oil as the hatch opened. The coyote's body shielded Hatch from the light pouring in the tunnel, bathing the once darkened surroundings in its pale glow. It took only a few moments for Hatch's eyes to adjust to the brightness.

A long-haired, leather-faced man stared down the hole at Hatch. He then assaulted the coyote in a barrage of rapid Spanish. Hatch was worried the lid was going to come crashing down on her and the man who'd brought her here. Instinctively, her hand drifted back to the weapon tucked against the small of her back.

The coyote returned a volley of Spanish. The argument ended when the coyote tossed the cash-filled envelope out. The gatekeeper's long greasy hair flopped over his tanned face when he ducked to catch it. If Hatch were looking to kill these men, now would've been the perfect time. But she didn't. She waited.

WHITEWATER: CHAPTER THREE

The coyote went first. Hatch half expected them to close the lid on her, but apparently the money in her pocket held more value than her life. She recognized the glint in the long-haired smuggler's eyes held a different intention, a lustful one, that may have contributed to his concession. Neither reason mattered. Hatch was now out of the tunnel and standing on Mexican soil.

The room was empty of people, aside from the two smugglers. The space had once been a cheaply designed bar, long since abandoned. A table nearby was covered in empty, and some not-so empty, beer bottles. A half-eaten plate of beans and rice showed their arrival had interrupted the greasy one's dinner.

The two smugglers were shoulder to shoulder, blocking Hatch from the only door she saw. She towered five inches over both men. The coyote's right hand drifted toward the revolver on his hip.

"Don't go for yours and I won't go for mine."

It seemed to take the men a second to realize that she had a gun of her own and that it was in her hand behind her back.

The coyote threw his hands up. The broken smile, worse in the light, reappeared. "Easy, pretty lady. This is just business."

Hatch slid her filth-covered right hand along the seam of her pants to the cargo pocket containing the rest of the promised money. Hatch had another more sizable pouch of cash strapped along her ankle that she had no intention of sharing. The two men didn't move as Hatch retrieved the envelope. The brown stains from her encounter in the tunnel marked the white surface of the paper. She handed it over and the long-haired smuggler greedily snatched it up.

"Anything else you need?" The coyote asked.

"Did you two move a girl through here within the last day?"

The two men laughed, but it was the greasy haired man who spoke. "We run girls through here all the time."

" Red hair, pale skin. Around seventeen years old?" Hatch stared at them with her hand firmly rooted against the gun. "Ring any bells?"

"No."

"There's money in it if you did." Hatch wouldn't pay that fee though.

If she got a sniff that these two were involved in the abduction and transport of Angela Rothman, Hatch would extract the information in a more brutal way.

"As much as I'd like to take your money, still no. And if she was anything like you, I'd remember."

Hatch read both men. As despicable as they were, neither gave any indication that they'd had any contact with the teen.

Hatch stepped forward, and the two men parted. Her shoulder forced the greasy-haired smuggler back, almost causing him to drop the cash he was counting as she made her way to the door.

Hatch stepped out in the warm night air. It smelled like a sewer line had broken nearby, but better than the hundred feet of tunnel she'd crossed to get here. She hoped to find some help, but first she needed to find a change of clothes and a place to wash the filth from her.

Pre-order *Whitewater (Rachel Hatch Book Six)* now:
https://www.amazon.com/gp/product/B08P27ZT4P

ALSO BY L.T. RYAN

Visit https://ltryan.com/pb for paperback purchasing information.

The Jack Noble Series

The Recruit (Short Story)
The First Deception (Prequel 1)
Noble Beginnings (Jack Noble #1)
A Deadly Distance (Jack Noble #2)
Thin Line (Jack Noble #3)
Noble Intentions (Jack Noble #4)
When Dead in Greece (Jack Noble #5)
Noble Retribution (Jack Noble #6)
Noble Betrayal (Jack Noble #7)
Never Go Home (Jack Noble #8)
Beyond Betrayal (Clarissa Abbot)
Noble Judgment (Jack Noble #9)
Never Cry Mercy (Jack Noble #10)
Deadline (Jack Noble #11)
End Game (Jack Noble #12)
Noble Ultimatum (Jack Noble #13) - Spring 2021

Bear Logan Series

Ripple Effect

Blowback

Take Down

Deep State

Rachel Hatch Series

Drift

Downburst

Fever Burn

Smoke Signal

Firewalk - December 2020

Whitewater - March 2021

Mitch Tanner Series

The Depth of Darkness

Into The Darkness

Deliver Us From Darkness - coming Summer 2021

Cassie Quinn Series

Path of Bones

Untitled - February, 2021

Blake Brier Series

Unmasked

Unleashed - January, 2021

Untitled - April, 2021

Affliction Z Series

Affliction Z: Patient Zero
Affliction Z: Abandoned Hope
Affliction Z: Descended in Blood
Affliction Z: Fractured (Part 1)
Affliction Z: Fractured (Part 2) - October, 2021

ABOUT THE AUTHOR

L.T. RYAN is a *USA Today* and Amazon bestselling author. The new age of publishing offered L.T. the opportunity to blend his passions for creating, marketing, and technology to reach audiences with his popular Jack Noble series.

Living in central Virginia with his wife, the youngest of his three daughters, and their three dogs, L.T. enjoys staring out his window at the trees and mountains while he should be writing, as well as reading, hiking, running, and playing with gadgets. See what he's up to at ltryan.com.

BOOKS IN THE JACK NOBLE SERIES

The Recruit (prequel short story)
The First Deception (prequel)
Noble Beginnings
A Deadly Distance
Thin Line
Noble Intentions
When Dead in Greece
Noble Retribution
Noble Betrayal
Never Go Home
Noble Judgment
Never Cry Mercy
Deadline
End Game

BOOKS IN THE BEAR LOGAN SERIES
Ripple Effect
Blowback
Takedown
Deep State (coming January, 2020)

BOOKS IN THE CLARISSA ABBOT SERIES
Beyond Betrayal

BOOKS IN THE MITCH TANNER SERIES
The Depths of Darkness
Into the Darkness
Deliver Us From Darkness (coming soon)

Social Media Links

Facebook (L.T. Ryan): facebook.com/LTRyanAuthor
    Facebook (Jack Noble Page): facebook.com/JackNobleBooks/
    Twitter: twitter.com/LTRyanWrites
    Goodreads: goodreads.com/author/show/6151659.L_T_Ryan

Contact L.T. Ryan at contact@ltryan.com

Printed in Great Britain
by Amazon